MW00438449

A Red Dress

Murder in the Green Mountain State

To Tim,

Enjoy,
August 28, 2021

[signature]

G.L Taylor

BookBaby Publishing
7905 N Crescent Blvd
Pennsauken Township, NJ 08110
www.bookbaby.com

Ordering Information:
For details, contact gary.taylor1750@gmail.com

Print ISBN: 978-1-09833-556-4
eBook ISBN: 978-1-09833-557-1

Printed in the United States of America on SFI Certified paper.

First Edition

I dedicate this book to my wife, Tammy,
for convincing me to write it,
and to each of the many hardworking police officers,
detectives, and prosecutors,
who worked tirelessly on the investigation mentioned in this book.

TABLE OF CONTENTS

INTRODUCTION

THIS BOOK IS A MEMOIR AND A HISTORICAL FICTION. IT IS BASED on a true story—an actual crime that occurred in a quaint and peaceful Vermont community on an early spring day in 1981. The attack left one girl dead and the other fighting for her life, while the entire state of Vermont was left shocked and aghast by this crime.

The reader will learn about the brutal attack on two twelve-year-old girls in a quintessential community park, and then accompany police officer Ben Fields and his fellow officers on the journey to solve the crime and apprehend the suspect(s).

Some of the names and identifying details have been changed to protect the privacy of individuals. This is a work of fiction. Names, characters, businesses, places, events and locales are either the products of the author's imagination or carefully blended with real names to substantiate the credibility of this story.

The author is represented in this story as Officer Ben Fields. Although Officer Ben Fields is a fictitious character created by the author, the author is a real person who spent forty-six years working as a police officer, a detective and a police commander, and finished his career as an accomplished police chief in northern Vermont. This story is told from the author's perspective, based on his role and participation in the criminal investigation from start to the finish.

This book contains material from the world in which we live, including references to actual places, people, and events, but it must be read as a work of historical fiction. Some of the dialogue is invented.

The fictitious names in this story represent real people, and the "key" is the relationship between the nonfiction and the fiction.

This book is a must-read for Vermonters and all true crime story buffs.

1

I WAS SOUND ASLEEP, WHEN MY WIFE, CAROL, CAME INTO THE bedroom and woke me up. The clock beside the bed showed 9:15 am. She said that Sgt. Bedard from the Station was on the telephone for me.

I took the phone, and Sgt. Bedard said, "Fields, I need you to come in to work an hour early. Officer Cahill, who was on the dayshift, went home sick, leaving the dayshift short one officer." Sgt. Bedard told me that he would cover most of the shift shortage, but that he had a prior commitment at 3 pm and had to leave by 2:45 pm, at the latest.

I was scheduled on shift at 4 pm this afternoon, so I would have to plan to be at the station to start my shift at 3 pm. Ah hell, a little overtime was always good. I would take whatever I could get. I had a reputation for being a bit of a workaholic, and everyone knew that I regularly jumped at the opportunity to work overtime.

Back then, I made one-hundred-seventy-nine dollars a week. That was before taxes. I was married and had two young children. It took everything I earned just to pay the bills and put food on the table.

I agreed to come in early, and told Sergeant Bedard that I would see him at 3 pm. I lived in Waynesville—had lived there since I was in the 7th grade.

Now that I was already awake, I got dressed and came out of the bedroom. As I entered the kitchen, Carol handed me yesterday's mail, which normally arrived between 4 and 5 pm daily, but usually after I had left for work when I worked the mid-shift.

I glanced through the envelopes and noted that they were mostly monthly bills and the run-of-the-mill junk mail, except for one envelope. It was addressed to Cpl. Ben Fields, Waterford Police Department, but had my home mailing address on it.

I had been waiting for the notification of the final results of the promotional process. It had included submitting a resume, a personnel file performance review, a Chief's interview, and an Oral Board. I had applied for an open detective's position.

Applicants had to have been a full-time police officer in good standing for at least four years to even apply. I generally received official police department mail at work, not at home. I tore the envelope open, wondering if it could be what I hoped it was.

Inside, I found a very official-looking letter, written on police department stationary, signed by the Waterford Police Chief.

It was addressed to me: Cpl. Ben Fields, and read:

> 'Thank you for your recent participation in the promotional process for detective. I am pleased to announce that you have been selected to be promoted to Detective Cpl., and reassigned to the Criminal Investigation Division, effective July 1, 1981. You have a proven track record, and this promotion is well-deserved.
>
> Congratulations. Signed, 'Chief Terrance Whitmore'.

I was ecstatic. I was whooping and hopping around when the kids rushed into the kitchen from the other room. They started hopping around and clapping their hands too, even though they had no idea why we were all doing it.

Annie kept asking, "What Daddy?" I told her, and my son, Jared, that it meant that I would be mostly working days during the week, so that I would have weekends and holidays off, and I would be home most nights when they went to bed, so I could tuck them in at bedtime. They liked the sound of that.

I had spent the past seven years on the job jockeying a marked patrol car, working shifts that changed every month. One month, I worked days, the next month, I rotated to the midnight shift, and the third month, I rotated to the mid-shift, from 4 pm to midnight. Then it started all over again.

I had set my sights on becoming a detective shortly after beginning my career as a police officer. I was very ambitious and a people person. I felt like I could make a difference. I was dedicated, and felt a special calling to this line of work. I felt like if I worked hard and solved criminal cases, I could make a greater contribution to police work in general, and then work on more serious calls and bigger criminal investigations.

At the first municipal police department that I worked for, the Middleton Falls Police Department, I had worked on a joint major drug investigation case with the federal Drug Enforcement Administration. It involved a local pilot named Winn Richardson, who was working as a private airplane pilot and smuggling large amounts of cocaine into the Banbury International Airport on a weekly basis. Half of the load went to a bar and nightclub named Johnny P's, in Middleton Falls.

We had learned that the drug shipment went directly into the cellar of the bar, where it was cut and stepped on. The cellar was also where all of the drink pre-mixer tanks were located and piped up to the bar: Tom Collins, Tonic, Half and half, gingerale, Coca Cola, etc.

One day, I posed as the driver's helper on the delivery at Johnny P's—official deliveryman uniform and all. I helped the regular driver carry all the full pre-mix tanks in and the empty tanks out. I managed to get a good look around the basement, and later, drew the basement layout, with its three separate rooms and a barely maintained bathroom, back at the police station. That drawing proved to be very valuable during the raid operation planning phase of the investigation.

I worked in an undercover capacity on two other separate occasions during the investigation. On one of those occasions, I assumed the role of a parcel express delivery driver. We (the police) had obtained a no-knock search warrant for one of Mr. Richardson's illicit drug associates, and I drove the Tactical Team secreted in the rear of the parcel express delivery vehicle up to the residence.

We had placed bricks in a twenty-four by twelve-inch box. Just space enough for nine bricks, which made the box fairly heavy. We then placed that box in another box that was thirty-six inches by twenty-four inches, stuffed packing beans around the two boxes, and sealed them inside one another. We affixed a delivery label addressed to the home occupant on the top of the box, just in case he wanted to make sure the package was for him.

I pulled into the driveway, exited the delivery truck, and carried the package to the front door. I was wearing an official parcel express uniform. I rang the doorbell and waited for the suspect to answer the door. When he answered, I explained that I had a package for him. I held the box while he signed my delivery slip using the box as a base to write on. He handed me the signed slip and I handed him the package. It was deliberately heavy and large, requiring him to use both hands to take the package from me.

I had parked the delivery truck just far enough from the front door, enabling the Tactical Team to exit the truck quietly through the front passenger door, and assemble in their pre-planned stack, against the front of the closed garage door.

When the suspect took the package and turned away to carry it into his home, I held the door open, and without him ever even noticing, the swift-moving Tactical Team entered his home right behind him. He was startled by them, and surprised by their announcement that they were the police and that they had a court-ordered search warrant for his home.

The low-profile take-down, coupled with the drugs and related drug evidence the Tactical Team found in his home provided a perfect opportunity for the team leaders to flip him. He admitted his role in the cocaine smuggling, receiving and distribution case. He negotiated with the DEA Agents for their support and testimony about his help on this case when it went to the Grand Jury, and he further agreed to cooperate and be a Confidential Informant (C.I.) while the investigation continued.

On the third occasion, I posed as a telephone lineman working in a utility bucket truck, forty-five feet above the ground. My job was to obtain video and still photos of the suspects unloading cocaine from Winn

Richardson's Suburban and carrying it into Johnny P's. I spent four and a half hours in that utility bucket, before obtaining the evidentiary photos that would be used to establish a legal nexus between Richardson and Johnny P's.

I worked on this case for seven months with two other Middleton Falls police investigators and three Drug Enforcement Agents (DEA). During that operation, I realized that I really wanted to be a detective and a criminal drug investigator. Even after leaving the Middleton Falls Police Department and joining the Waterford Police Department for better pay and benefits, I was still striving to be promoted to detective. This was the opportunity that I had been working so hard to obtain.

I wasn't suggesting that the work done by patrol officers wasn't valuable or important, because I believed then and still do today, that they are the backbone of any police department. They are always the first police officers, and first responders, for that matter, on the scene, and the last to clear. They are often faced with tragic and dangerous situations, and they clear the way for the rest of us to come in safely.

In a small town like Waterford, patrol officers do spend a lot of their time helping the younger school kids cross at the Five Corners as they walk to and from school each day, looking for missing and lost children, answering barking dog complaints, and providing information to community visitors. Additionally, the day shift patrol officers were required to deliver arrest cases and court paperwork to the State's Attorney's office in neighboring Banbury every day, write parking tickets, and create a visible presence in the communities sprawling neighborhoods, both in patrol cars and on foot beats.

Stopping illicit drug dealers from distributing their poison to the young and innocent, the addicted and the vulnerable, at-risk adults looking for some adventure and release, was one of my top priorities. I felt strongly about interrupting, dismantling and arresting the lowlifes and predators, who were getting rich off of other people's addiction and agony. In many of these cases, the strongest among these people preyed on the weakest, sucking the very life out of their customers.

I also wanted to stop or solve serious crimes—crimes that change people's lives. That's why I had chosen the profession in the first place, and that's what I wanted to do now.

There is no doubt that there is a connection between illicit drug use, sales and trafficking and property crimes, such as thefts, frauds, robberies and burglaries. In the early stages of addiction, addicts are often unable to hold down any job because of their inconsistent behavior, inability to complete assigned tasks, or poor work attendance record, so they run out of money.

With the loss of their income, the addicts can't afford the cost of purchasing the supply that they feel they so desperately need. So, they steal from friends and relatives to get the money to purchase their fix. Addicts use and take advantage of their loved ones and friends, and often have no social support group besides their fellow addicts.

They always convince themselves that they are really just "borrowing" the money, fully intending to repay the person they stole or borrowed from. Then they realize that every time they have the money to repay their debt, they also need their drug of choice again. It's a vicious circle. When faced with competing choices, the addicts will most often act to satisfy their personal drug habit. After a while, no one will loan them any money, and everyone who has been victimized by them, starts locking everything up and refusing to help, because they know that the borrower will buy more drugs with it.

That is usually the stage where the addicts start committing crimes. Petty crimes at first, but over time, the crimes become bigger and bigger and more serious. In the more extreme cases, the addict may even become physically violent or aggressive towards others, opening the door to domestic violence, assault, assault and robberies, reckless and dangerous behavior, or conduct that places themselves and others in great danger, etc.

Since joining the Waterford Police Department, I had worked hard and put in some long hours to prove my investigative skills. I had signed up for and attended a variety of criminal investigation training courses in and out of the state of Vermont over the past year, and I had pulled extra duty working with department investigators, who were always conducting covert, criminal drug investigations and following up on commercial and residential burglaries, armed robberies and sexual assaults.

As the excitement over my promotion began to subside, I realized that I still had several hours before I had to be at work. I grabbed my morning coffee, and joined Jared and Annie, who had returned to playing a children's game called 'Operation' on the living room floor. As I drank my morning coffee, I playfully joked with them about their patient's prognosis, after having all of his most important parts removed from his body.

"It's good practice. You'll develop steady hands, so when you go to medical school, you'll already have what it takes to operate on people," I said, as I chuckled a little.

We all laughed at that, and my son, Jared, who was six years old, said, "I don't want to be a doctor when I grow up Dad. I'm going to be a policeman, just like you." He jumped up off the floor, came over to me, and patted my leg proudly as he said it.

My daughter, Annie, who was eight years old, chimed in and said, "Me too." I assured them that they could both be police officers when they grew up—if that is what they wanted to be. But there was still plenty of time for them to play 'Operation' and do all of the things that kids do when they're growing up. "There's plenty of time to figure all of that out later," I said, ending the conversation.

Annie was a pretty little thing with long, blonde hair—she was quite girlish. Jared looked like a smaller, younger version of me. He was boisterous like all young boys, and could be a real handful sometimes.

I showered and changed for work at 2 pm. It was a twenty-minute ride to work and I didn't want to be late, especially since I had just received my promotion notice.

Before I went out of the door, there was a round of hugs and kisses. Annie hugged me and kissed me goodbye, and said, "Watch out for those bad guys, Dad." Annie said this every day, when I left for work.

Lately, Jared had started imitating Annie, and saying, "Get the bad guys, Dad," with a very serious look on his face. I guess he didn't want me to think that his sister cared more about my job, than he did.

We always parted with a high five, and I assured them that I would "get those bad guys." I never left for work without saying 'I love you' to each of them, except of course, when I worked midnights because they were already in bed when I left the house. But I still made it a point to tell them I loved them when I tucked them into bed and read them a bedtime story.

They loved having me read to them before they went to sleep. When I read a story to them, I would always ad-lib and insert fun, little things that were not really in the book. It was our little game. They were always on guard and whenever I would do it, they would catch me. Most of the time, it was Annie who would say, "Dad, that's not in the book." I would say, "But it makes the story better, doesn't it?" She would smile, and say, "No, Dad. You are just supposed to read the words in the book." I would always give up after some light-hearted play between us. I'd say, "Okay, then," and proceed to read the book the way it was written.

Most of the time when I ad-libbed, I would say things like, "... and then a platypus wandered into the backyard," or sometimes, I would say, "... and then a rhinoceros or a giraffe knocked on the front door." Something exaggerated, just for a laugh.

This was my way of injecting some humor and playfulness into my quality time with Annie and Jared. Life is too serious and stressful, and children should be happy and spend most of their time laughing and playing. Kids need to be kids.

2

It was Friday, May 15, 1981, and it was a typical spring day in Vermont. It was just warm enough not to need a coat, but raining off and on, so that it was necessary to wear a windbreaker or a light raincoat.

The light rain didn't bother me much because we were still in our winter uniforms, which were long-sleeved shirts. I felt that the long sleeves on my duty shirt would protect me from the raindrops on today's shift, without the need for a jacket. We were not scheduled to change out our uniform shirts to short sleeves until Memorial Day weekend.

I enjoyed the ride from my home in Waynesville, which was only one town away from Waterford, where I worked. The drive-in was uneventful. I drove with my window down slightly so that I could enjoy the warmer spring weather. By this time of year, most of the population in

Vermont develops cabin fever, and is ready to welcome the nicer weather. So, on that day, most people were happy not to see any more snow until late fall, or early winter again—no more winter hats, gloves and boots for a few months. Not to mention, not having to shovel snow, or snow blow the driveway.

I arrived at the station at 2:45 pm, and went to work reading the police log, going through the mandatory cruiser checklist, and setting my cruiser up before the start of my shift, so that I was ready to start answering calls, if needed, right at shift change.

Police officers have the choice to change into uniform at the station, before and after their shift, or simply wear their uniform to and from work.

I always changed into it before I left the house, arriving and leaving work in uniform. That way, when I arrived at the police station for my shift, I was ready to go to work. Because as it always happens, when you are the least prepared for a hot call or a busy shift, that is when one will come in.

I was still thinking about Jared and Annie. I was trying to come up with a surprise family outing or activity for my fast-approaching six-day break. I had been entertaining the idea of taking them to the Wild Kingdom & Fun Park in the neighboring state of New York.

After all, it was only a three-and-a-half-hour ride to our west. There was a big water park just down the street from the theme park as well. I was already imagining the surprised look on their faces and the squeals of delight when I told them about it.

The Waterford Police Department comprised nineteen full-time police officers including me, and our jurisdiction covered forty-two square miles. We patrolled two communities—Waterford Village and the Town of Waterford. Combined, our jurisdiction's population was 20,000 residents and a large number of daily visitors, employees, and vendors, who worked in one of the many commercial business establishments, schools, or manufacturing facilities in town.

At that time, our department was considered a medium-sized police department here in the state of Vermont. Our community was located in Neary County.

I always believed Neary County was one of the nicest areas in Vermont to raise a family. Aside from my personal bias due to having grown up here, I felt lucky to live and work here. Our county had great schools, an abundance of bike and walking paths, hiking trails, lakefront beaches, and a wide variety of eateries, movie theaters, and an outdoor drive-in movie theater. Half of the entire state's population either lived in Neary County or worked here.

There were only one thousand police officers in the entire state of Vermont at that time, and police departments were far and few between in other parts of the state. There were fourteen police departments in Neary County, but once you left this immediate area, most of the state was fairly rural. In some of those rural areas, there were small police departments, with fewer than six officers.

The most rural communities in Vermont depended on the Vermont State Police, or in a few isolated cases, the County Sheriff's office, for police coverage. It was not uncommon for police departments in Vermont to have prearranged mutual aid agreements, or to simply offer assistance to one another when help was needed.

Waterford was home to the Kimball Bowley Corporation, also known worldwide by its acronym KBC, which at the time, was the largest computer manufacturer in the world. My mother worked for KBC, and had done so for twenty years now. She was one of twelve thousand employees and vendors who worked at the Waterford site daily. KBC's computer business facility and the manufacturing campus were located on more than five hundred acres of land in Waterford Village, with dozens of offices, buildings, and warehouses scattered across it.

KBC had offices and production sites in Canada, Germany, Ireland, and in several states in the United States. Waterford Town and Village residents and local politicians alike, routinely bragged about the fact that KBC called Waterford, Vermont, their home manufacturing base.

The KBC campus was impressive by any measure. They owned and operated their own sewage treatment, water, and electrical facilities, had their own on-site security force, fire department, rescue squad and medical facility. Their campus was a community within a community.

Waterford was also home to ten separate elementary and junior high school campuses, spread throughout the Town and Village, and had one of the largest regional high schools and technical centers in our region. The high school's and technical center's combined student and staff population numbered 1,800.

3

I WAS SCHEDULED TO WORK THE MID-SHIFT TODAY WITH TWO OTHER police officers—Officer Bill Killen and Officer Jeremy Jones. The three of us were gathered in the squad room conducting our version of the 'roll call,' and updating each other on some recent criminal trends and incidents in our community that would require some extra attention. This information was gleaned from the police log or typed notes left on the roll call clipboard by the previous shift.

In between the serious topics, we light-heartedly made comments about wanting to have a quiet shift. Looking back now, I realize that making statements like that are foolish, and it is always considered taboo in police work. Even police officers who are not superstitious believe that they will jinx themselves when they make these kinds of statements, and this time was no exception. This shift would prove to be anything but quiet.

Police officers live by the rule of three. Rule 1: A full moon is always bad news. Rule 2: Deaths and death investigations come in waves of three. Rule 3: Making comments about a quiet shift will usually bring just the opposite.

Officer Killen was starting days off tomorrow and he had been planning a brook trout fishing expedition that he was excited about. He and two of his friends were going to fish a fourteen-mile section of the Neary Brook. They planned to be casting lines into the water by 6:30 am tomorrow morning.

My days off were still two days away, and Officer Jones had just returned to work after having had three days off. He proudly announced that he had spent his time off lounging around the house without ever changing out of his pajamas—doing nothing but lying around and watching television. — exactly what he preferred to do when the opportunity presented itself.

The squad room at the police station was filled with desks, file cabinets, two wall-mounted dry-erase boards, and two folding tables pushed together in the middle of the room, to create a large, makeshift conference room table. This provided the officers with work, break and meal space, out of the public's watch. It's hard to relax at all when an officer tries to grab a bite in public. Everyone is watching the person in uniform.

The squad room was adjacent to the dispatch center, with only a door separating the two rooms. Today, like most days, the door between the two rooms was open, for improved air circulation and oral communications between the dispatch center and the officers in the office.

Leaving the door open also made the dispatchers feel less isolated and closed off from the on-duty police officers, who were frequently in and out of the squad room, picking up forms, or writing reports, etc., during their shifts.

Waterford Village and Town were broken into three distinct Patrol Zones. All three zones blended overlapping patrol areas in the Village and the Town. Officers were responsible for all primary calls in their assigned zone, as well as for conducting routine patrol in their assigned zone, when not answering calls.

Patrol Zone 1 was the busiest. It was in the heart of the downtown region of the two communities. Zones 2 and 3 were larger geographical areas, but received fewer police calls. When a shift was short on officers, we would sometimes combine Zone 2 and 3, and have one patrol officer cover both zones. That was unnecessary today. We had three officers on shift, and we would each take a separate zone. In the interest of being fair and equitable in the distribution of the workload, officers would swap patrol areas halfway through their shift. This was mostly because Zone 1 was so much busier than Zones 2 and 3.

When no Patrol Supervisor was working on shift—which was the case today—the officers working on the shift would mutually decide who would cover each zone. Once decided, the dispatchers on-duty would be informed, so that he or she could assign calls to the appropriate officers and track each officer's status and availability for the next call.

If a call was received in your zone, you were the primary officer assigned, even if other officers responded as well. Any additional officers on or at your call, were there to assist you. You managed your cases and were responsible for investigating the incidents that happened in your assigned area. This included making all of the decisions about that case. You were also responsible for any of the related paperwork, notifications, and follow-up.

During today's roll-call, we had decided that I would be in Zone 2 for the first four hours of my shift and Killen would be in Zone 1, with Jones covering Zone 3. Halfway through our shift, Killen and I would swap patrol zones. I would move to Zone 1 and he would move to Zone 2. Jones would remain in Zone 3 for the entire shift.

Sometimes, when there were no supervisors or command staff on shift, and a dispatcher would call to see where a given officer was, some of the officers would jokingly tell the dispatchers they were in the O-Zone or the Twilight Zone. It was just an inside joke to lighten things up a little.

At 4:30 pm, the three of us were in the process of leaving the station to go out on patrol when we heard the telephone ringing in the dispatch center. By the second ring, dispatcher Lois Carter had answered the call. "Waterford Police Department," she said, listening intently and a serious look coming over her face. She started to speak louder, asking very specific questions.

Police officers can very often tell how bad or how serious a call is by the volume and tone of the dispatcher's voice, either in person or over the police radio.

"Can I get your name again, please? Where did you say she is? Can you say that again?" Do you know how old she is?" As her voice became louder and more intense, she seemed anxious, or perhaps upset.

She covered the mouthpiece of the phone and quickly shouted to the three of us to wait a minute. She returned to the caller briefly, before turning back to us to say, "I have a caller reporting that a young girl has been found on the railroad tracks. She is naked and bleeding badly. The caller is reporting that she is conscious and mumbling. He believes, from her appearance and her mumblings, that she may have been raped."

The dispatcher said that the man who found her was a railroad employee and he was going to walk the victim to an area along the railroad tracks, near the intersection of Maple and Elm Street. I will never forget the expression on her face, as we rushed for the back door—it was an expression of shock and horror.

Officers Killen, Jones, and I ran out the back door and hopped into our cruisers. With emergency lights on and sirens wailing, we raced from the police station parking lot towards the intersection of Maple and Elm Street.

The Maple and Elm Street intersection was in Zone II, so I already knew that I would be the primary officer in this case. This meant that the case would be assigned to me, and I would be responsible for managing the police department's response, calling for further assistance, or specialty officers if needed, and at the very minimum, conducting the initial investigation. I would be required to prepare and manage any of the related paperwork, not that any of that was important right now.

The traffic was heavy because of the shift change at KBC. The route we had to take to get to Maple and Elm Street, where we were meeting the victim and the man escorting her, was the same route that employees driving to and from their job at KBC took every day.

We carefully made our way through the Five Corners, which was always daunting at that time of the day. We weaved in and out of traffic, intent on getting there as quickly as possible. As I maneuvered from one lane to the other, my mind raced with thoughts about what to expect when I arrived.

Could this really be happening? Who would do such a thing? How bad would this call be? Who would I need to notify or call in?

The rush of adrenalin coursing through my body, as the sirens on our police cars wailed, combined with the nature of this call, made my heart race. Most police officers become adrenalin junkies during their first year on the job. During training at the police academy, we had been taught to control our breathing, to slow our pulse rate during moments like this. I reminded myself to take long, deep breaths.

Officers Killen, Jones and I, all arrived at the intersection of Elm and Maple Streets at about the same time. We pulled our cruisers off to the side of the road, and quickly hopped out of them, jogging towards the railroad tracks, where I could see an older man, whose name I later learned was Henry Thompson, and a small girl—whose name I would never forget—walking towards me.

Mr. Thompson was walking straight towards me with the small girl at his side. He had his hands on her shoulder—as if he was holding her up as they walked. Even though I would later recall hearing the dispatcher say that the caller reported that the girl was naked and bleeding, when I first spotted her, I thought she was wearing a red dress, because she was so uniformly covered in blood from her neck down to her knees. As I approached Mr. Thompson and the little girl, I could see that she was, in fact, naked, and the blood she was covered in, appeared to be her own. It was coming from wounds to her neck and what appeared to be stab wounds to her chest.

I knelt in front of her, and asked what her name was. She said, "Wendy Redding." Her voice crackled and was barely above a whisper. It was very weak. My first responder, emergency medical training had taught me that these were strong indications that Wendy was in shock, or about to be.

I told her that medical help was on the way. Now my heart started racing again, and my first thought was, "Oh my God, who could have done this?" I could see that Wendy had sustained at least one, possibly two, stab wounds to the chest that were still bleeding badly. One of the stab wounds must have punctured her lung because as she tried to breathe, blood bubbles were exuding from the wound. In medical terms, this is referred to as a 'sucking chest wound'. A sucking chest wound (SCW) happens when an injury causes a hole to open in your chest and lung, it is often caused by stabbing, gunshots, or other injuries that penetrate the chest.

I could also see that her throat had been slashed with a sharp instrument several times. She was bleeding profusely from those neck injuries. I found it unbelievable that Wendy was conscious and still walking around with such serious injuries.

I tried to convince her to lie down on the ground, but she insisted on sitting upright, on a wooden guardrail that ran along the side of the railroad tracks. Wendy had a strange look in her eyes. Her pupils were fixed, and she had a blank stare, even when she was looking directly at me. It was almost as if she was looking right through me and everyone else gathered around her.

As I was trying to comfort and reassure her, she tried to tell me something that I could barely hear. I leaned in close to her and asked her to repeat what she had said. Through that still-raspy voice, I heard her say that her friend was still in the woods and that her friend was hurt even worse than she (Wendy) was. When I asked her to tell me her friend's name, she said, "Stacie". It was barely audible. Wendy seemed to be drifting off, so I quickly followed up by asking her where we could find her friend, Stacie.

Wendy's breathing had become labored and more sporadic now, and the air bubbles being exuded from her chest wound seemed to be growing larger. Wendy didn't speak this time. She simply pointed south down the railroad tracks.

The older man, Henry Thompson, who was with Wendy, identified himself as a railroad employee—a train conductor, who was riding in the caboose of a passing train. He said that he had spotted Wendy staggering down a well-worn footpath through the woods, at the back of the Johnson Street Park that leads to the railroad tracks.

Mr. Thompson said that the moment he saw her, he shouted to the train engineer on his portable radio, and told him to call the police. Mr. Thompson then said that he jumped off from the slow-moving train and ran to the little girl. He added that he tried to help her by holding her upright and walking her to where she could more readily receive help. He said that he had offered to carry her, but that she was insistent that she could walk.

Mr. Thompson said that the train engineer relayed all of his information to their train dispatcher, who in turn called the police. Mr. Thompson was very choked up, but he went on to try and provide a more detailed description of the well-worn footpath, where he had initially spotted Wendy.

He said that he believed that the footpath ran from the railroad tracks to the back of the Johnson Street Park. He said that he believed that the local kids used it as a short-cut to certain parts of the community. Then, almost as an afterthought, he said, "That might be where Wendy's friend is."

Mr. Thompson would tell us in a subsequent interview that this was one of the regular train routes that he traveled on, as a part of his job with the railroad, adding that he would often see kids walking from that path towards the railroad tracks, or the railroad tracks onto the path, into the park, when passing by.

By now, first responders and Waterford Rescue Squad members were arriving on the scene. They immediately went to work attending to Wendy, with a determined focus. I watched them tape a piece of plastic over the bubbling chest wound and wrap gauze around Wendy's neck wounds.

Once I was satisfied that Wendy was in good hands, I set out to try and find Stacie, Wendy's missing girlfriend—the girl that Wendy had told us was hurt worse than she was, and who was still in the woods.

Officers Killen, Jones, and I ran south for almost three-quarters of a mile along the railroad tracks, before we found the footpath near the back of Johnson Street Park where Mr. Thompson had indicated he had found Wendy. Just as he had described, there was a well-established footpath leading from the railroad tracks to the back of the Johnson Street Park. We quickly discovered that the path into the park split into a 'V' and became two paths, within the first one hundred feet. We would later confirm that both paths lead into the back area of the park, but each comes out in a different location inside the park.

At about this same time, we encountered an older, white-haired man, walking near the path by the railroad tracks. He walked right up to me and asked what we were looking for. I told him that we were looking for a young, injured girl, who was last known to be in this general vicinity. He said that he hadn't seen anyone fitting that description, but he offered to help us search. I told him that if he was going to remain in the area, he should call out if he saw, or found anything, which he agreed to do.

Before walking away from him and just to be on the safe side, I quickly wrote his name and address down in my notebook, which I—like every other police officer—always carried in my back pocket. Police officers were required to carry notebooks, to write down important information, or make notes, so they wouldn't forget or so they could reference it when writing reports or when the officer was testifying in court.

Believing that time was of the essence and that this second young victim's health and safety may depend on our ability to find her as quickly as possible, and in the interest of not wanting to waste any more time discussing who would search where, I volunteered to search along the path on our left and Officers Killen and Jones agreed that they would search the path on the right.

The footpath was narrow and had been worn into the ground by individuals walking on it repeatedly over many years. In some areas, the tree limbs and outgrowth of brush overhung the path, making it even narrower and more difficult to push through.

Within a few minutes of searching the footpath that I was on, I discovered another less well-worn path on my right that I would later realize, connected the path that I was on with the path that Officers Killen and Jones were searching.

This cross-cut path was much less obvious and more obscure. It appeared to be used more infrequently than the original path, which would account for why it was so much less well-worn and hidden.

I concluded that if someone was not specifically looking for it or paying attention, they might not even notice it. This was an area away from the main path, with fewer people using it. I found myself thinking that a person committing this type of crime, in a public area like this, might choose a more private, remote area, that is better hidden from any passing foot traffic—this path provided that cover.

That's when I heard Officer Killen shout, "Over here". His voice was coming from right in front of me, on this second cross-cut path. They must have spotted this cross-cut path as they searched the other footpath and must have had thoughts similar to mine.

I pushed my way through the heavy brush and tree cover for more than three hundred feet, walking with difficulty to a small clearing where Killen and Jones we already standing. The clearing was small and appeared to be a local party site in the middle of the woods. Probably, carved out and used by underage area youth. It could not be seen while walking on either of the other two paths.

The clearing was strewn with discarded snack packages, empty potato chip bags, beer cans, and soda bottles. There were also two old and filthy single bed-sized, foam mattresses in the clearing. One of the mattresses was on my right side, against the tree line, as I entered the clearing, and the other mattress was on my left side, near some fallen tree limbs in the clearing.

The tree limbs appeared to have been dragged there and used to sit on—kind of a makeshift seating and campfire area.

There was a large burnt area on the ground from previous campfires, or a jerry-rigged firepit in front of the fallen tree limbs. It looked like someone had sat on the tree limbs, in front of a fire. There were several burned pieces of twigs and small charred tree limbs still lying in the burned area on the ground.

Both of the mattresses were disgusting, filthy, and heavily bloodstained. One of them appeared to have been tossed to its final resting place, on the left side of the clearing, closest to the campfire and tree limbs. When I looked at the other mattress, on the right side of the clearing, I could see two, small legs and a pair of small, bare feet protruding from beneath it.

My heart was pounding in my chest as I was trying to process what I was seeing. Who did this, and why? These are just little girls.

Officer Killen said that he had already checked the victim under the foam mattress for signs of life, but said he did not detect any. He then asked me to double-check and confirm his findings.

I rushed forward to the filthy mattress, got down on my knees and lifted one end of it. There on the ground, beneath the mattress was a small, girl, facedown with a knee sock tied around her head, through her mouth, like some makeshift bridle on a horse. This must be Stacie, the girlfriend that Wendy had told us about, who was still in the woods and hurt worse than her.

Stacie's hair was tangled into the knotted knee sock tied through her mouth. Her skin tone was ashen and her body was cool to my touch. I felt for a pulse in her carotid artery on her neck, but could not find one. I reached down and gently lifted her right shoulder off the ground, rolling her up onto her left side slightly, facing me, so that I could see her face and check for any other possible signs of life.

She was just a little girl, and if there was any hope of saving her, I wanted to make sure we didn't miss it. I'm not sure what I was looking for, but I knew that we had to do everything we could to try and save her if there was any possibility of it at all.

When I rolled her up on her left side, I could see that her throat had been slashed several times quite deeply, and her right eye was grossly disfigured. There was blood and fluid from her eye that had oozed down the right side of her face. She also had several gaping stab wounds to the center of her chest. The horrific image of Stacie was forever etched into my mind. I stared at her face and small body in disbelief.

After having found no pulse or any other signs of life, I realized there was nothing that we could do to try and save her young life. Not wanting to disrespect Stacie in any way, I gently laid her back down in the same position that I had found her in, allowing the foam mattress to fall back on top of her as we had found it. I then turned to Officers Killen and Jones, and confirmed that I had not found any signs of life either. The little girl was dead, just as Officer Killen had already observed.

Feeling sickened by that little girl's injuries, and the thought of what must have happened here, I stood up quickly and walked several yards away from the body, near a large pine tree. I hunched forward, feeling like I was going to be sick to my stomach. I gagged several times but did not vomit. I did, however, have the dry heaves. I stayed there until I recovered while thinking about the horrible atrocity that had occurred in this makeshift party or campsite.

Who did this to this child? What kind of a monster must they be? As I thought about it, I became mentally enraged. This little girl was the same size as my eight-year-old daughter, Annie. She was also about the same build and approximate age as Annie.

At about this time, I realized that it had started raining again. The raindrops were cool as they bounced off my head and face. I could hear voices blaring over my portable police radio requesting further information and location details. I don't remember which one of us answered the radio, but one of us did. We then transmitted back to the police station our location and case status for any other responding officers, or fire and rescue personnel.

Killen, Jones, and I stood there trying to take it all in. We looked around the crime scene at the various sights, making mental notes in anticipation of required reports and related paperwork.

I can still recall the smell of death in the air and the smell of the dirty mattresses. We just stood there, looking at one another in disbelief, with expressions of horror on all of our faces. Each one of us was trying to fathom exactly what had happened and who may have done this.

This was the first time that I had ever seen anything like this. It is the most horrific image I have ever seen—even to this day. I would go on to witness many more violent crime scenes and murder victims in my eventual forty-six-year police career, but none that would affect me permanently, like this.

I would go on to see enough pain, suffering, trauma, and death to last any normal person several lifetimes. Each case uniquely different from the last, but always ending with the tragic and often violent loss of human life… Each crime scene telling its own distinct, gruesome story about the cruel and evil things that human beings often do to one another…

The air was charged with the sounds of sirens, off in the distance coming closer and closer. My auditory senses were peaked and operating at maximum capability, picking up on every noise and sound within miles of our present location. I could hear the sounds of the raindrops hitting the leaves on the trees and on the ground. I heard a distant train whistle from afar, as it approached each of the many railroad grade crossings in the Town and Village of Waterford.

As equally odd as the acute sense of hearing, and even more unnerving, was the eerie silence immediately surrounding Killen, Jones and I, as we stood there in that clearing next to Stacie's lifeless body. No one had anything to say as we tried to comprehend what had happened here and what the next steps to be taken would be.

In the meantime, the older, white-haired gentleman, who I had first encountered by the railroad tracks, found his way to us. We heard him coming through the brush before we actually saw him. He was walking towards us, on the cross-cut footpath that this clearing was located on when Officer Jones intercepted him before he could make it into the clearing where we had found Stacie's body.

The old man asked if we had found what we were looking for. Officer Jones said that we had. The man then asked again if he could help in any way. Officer Jones said that he didn't think so, but he would check, as he turned and asked me what I thought. I told Jones that we could have him stand at the end of this cross-cut path where it intersects with the other footpath, so that he could help guide any other responding police officers, or rescue personnel to our location in this clearing. The older gentleman seemed eager to do this.

Before the helpful, older man took his position at his assigned post, and just as the rain began to fall even harder, he told us that he lived nearby and was going to run home and get a raincoat, but he would be right back. None of us had any problem with that whatsoever, but before he walked away, Officer Jones wrote his name and address down, in his police notebook, not realizing that I had already done the very same thing myself.

When I first encountered the old man and again when he was walking towards the crime scene on this footpath, I had visually scanned him from head to toe for blood, dirt, or any other sign that might make him a suspect in what had happened here, but there was nothing. As he left to walk to his nearby residence to retrieve his raincoat, Officers Killen, Jones, and I compared notes and speculated about the gentleman and his determined desire to help. We all agreed that he was no criminal, and we did not believe he had any part in what had happened here.

I radioed the on-duty dispatcher and requested that Detective Sgt. Bob Green be notified. I asked to have him respond directly to the crime scene. This was a major crime that would require advanced investigative skills, technical expertise, an experienced case manager, and someone with the authority to call in additional police personnel and resources.

We needed to cordon off and secure the crime scene perimeter itself, which I estimated might include the entire Johnson Street Park. There would have to be photographs taken, diagrams made, and evidence collected and processed. We needed to cover the crime scene to ensure that the rain did not distort or erase any evidence, and someone would need to go to the hospital immediately, if they hadn't already done so, to interview and guard the surviving victim, Wendy Redding. We needed to call for the Vermont State Police, Mobil Crime Lab to respond to the scene, as well as the Medical Examiner and the State's Attorney's office. And most importantly, we needed to identify the victim and notify her family about the facts and circumstances surrounding their daughter's death. Whoever the officer was that notified the next of kin would have to persuade a family member to agree to view the deceased victim and positively confirm her identity.

Once we had enough personnel, we would conduct a large-scale search of the park for any discarded evidence and locate any possible witnesses. We would also need investigators to track down and follow up on leads, as they developed.

Last, but not the least, someone would have to deal with the media. I was receiving reports that television news vans were lining up in the roadway, in front of the Johnson Street Park which was creating traffic problems. Additionally, I was receiving reports that individual news crews and reporters were traipsing through the woods, trying to find the crime scene. Word had gotten out that some type of tragedy had occurred in the park, and the press had no intention of being left out of any such breaking news.

Within a few minutes of being notified about the media traipsing through the woods, one of the very few perimeter officers that had already been deployed, Officer Blake Devoid, called over the radio to say that he had come across a reporter, David Peck, in the woods, a short distance away from the crime scene. Officer Devoid indicated that he was detaining him at their present location until further instructions.

David Peck was the most well-known crime reporter in Neary County or the entire state of Vermont, for that matter. He worked for a daily newspaper in Banbury called the *Banbury Daily News*, and according to Officer Devoid, he was determined to find his way to the crime scene.

Peck's reputation as an aggressive, never-takes-no-for-an-answer kind of reporter brought with it a host of concerns, not the least of which was that he would use his extensive list of police, dispatch and prosecutor contacts to obtain inside information about what had happened at the Johnson Street Park, and publish it before the State's Attorney, or investigative team, wanted the general public to know. It was equally critical—and the police department's duty—to protect the victims and crime information until the families of the victims and next of kin were notified.

Neary County State's Attorney, Jack Banfield, would later tell the media that he came very close to ordering David Peck's arrest, though he never did say what Peck would have been arrested for.

Officer Killen and I stayed with the deceased victim in that small clearing while Officer Jones left with our cruiser keys, and walked back to move our cruisers closer to the park. As we continued to quietly stand there, I remember thinking that I would never be able to rid my mind of today's images and this crime scene, in this beautiful park. I couldn't believe that someone could, or would, for that matter do such an evil thing. When I wasn't feeling sad for the girls, I was feeling outraged towards whoever did this.

The Johnson Street Park was surrounded by the small village of Waterford, which was only 4.2 square miles with 8,500 residents. The park was located directly across the street from one of the ten elementary school campuses in the community. This was a community where people didn't lock their cars or house doors… where residents let their kids walk to the store alone, or go to the neighborhood park, unescorted.

4

Detective Sgt. Bob Green arrived at the clearing in the woods within thirty minutes of being notified. After being shown around the crime scene and viewing Stacie's lifeless body and being told about *Banbury Daily News* reporter David Peck being detained in the woods, Sgt. Green asked me to step outside of the clearing so that he and I could speak privately for a minute.

When we were twenty feet or so from the clearing, and Officers Killen and Jones were no longer within earshot, he asked, "How are you doing? Are you holding up okay?" He added, "Let me know if you need anything." I agreed and promised to let him know if anything changed for me. Sgt. Green wasn't questioning my competency or my capabilities. We had become friends and he was trying to look out for me.

Three years ago, my wife and I had been friends with a married couple whose names were Nate and Birdie Wescott. They had a sixteen-year-old son, Arthur, who had sexually molested one of our daughter's best friends, at one of our next-door neighbor's homes, while the child's parents had gone out to dinner with the Wescotts.

We had been friends with the Wescotts for more than a year when the incident occurred. Birdie had always bragged about how mature and responsible her son, Arthur, was, and on more than one occasion, when they wanted us to go to dinner, or some other social function with them and we would say that we would have to see if we could get a babysitter for the kids, Birdie would offer Arthur as a babysitter.

I was not comfortable with the idea, and despite Birdie's reassurances and list of reputable families that Arthur had babysat for, I had held out, saying that I didn't think it was a good idea.

On this particular occasion, there was a planned birthday dinner arranged at a local restaurant for the husband of some mutual friends of ours. Our regular babysitter had already taken another babysitting job for the same evening with another one of the couples who planned to attend the dinner, so my wife, Carol, arranged for her mother, Rene, to watch our children.

Raymond and Clara Longway, the parents of Annie's best friend, Stephanie, were unable to find a sitter and were considering using Arthur. After a spirited debate between Carol, Birdie, the Longways and me about using Arthur to watch their daughter Stephanie and her younger brother, Roger, my logic seemed to fall on deaf ears, and the Longways decided to give Arthur a try. They would only be away from the house for two or three hours, they reasoned. Birdie, Raymond, Clara and Carol insisted this would be the perfect opportunity to give Arthur a chance.

We all went to dinner and had a wonderful time. I felt that I may have been a little heavy-handed with my staunch stance earlier in the evening about not allowing Arthur to watch Annie and Jared, or any other kids their age. Clara, Raymond, Birdie, Carol and Nate chided me a bit about my old-fashioned, sexist and chauvinistic attitude. I couldn't help myself. I felt strongly about how one can never be too careful when protecting and safeguarding young children. I did not think that a sixteen-year old boy should be babysitting young, prepubescent girls. Carol later told me that I had been obstinate and argumentative about Arthur watching Stephanie and Roger, but those kids were like part of my own family, and just as I didn't want anything bad to happen to our kids, I didn't want anything bad to happen to them either.

The next day, while I was at work, I was called in off the road by the on-duty dispatcher, who advised me that Police Chief Terrance Whitmore wanted to see me in his office immediately. I returned to the office, went to Chief Whitmore's office, and asked through the open door, "Chief, did you want to see me?" He said, "Yes. Come in and close the door." I did and he directed me to have a seat, so I sat down in a chair directly in front of his desk. Then he told me that I should call home right away—something had happened at my neighbor's house last night, involving Arthur Wescott. He said, "Everyone is okay now, but you need to call home and get the details from Carol."

The Chief then stood up and said use my phone, as he turned it on the desk so that it was facing me. He then exited his office and closed the door behind him. My heart was pounding in my chest as I grabbed the telephone and called home. Carol answered. "Carol," I said. "What's going on?" She immediately started crying, and said, "Last night, while we were all at dinner, Arthur sexually molested Annie's friend, Stephanie."

I asked, "What about Annie or Jared?" She said, "No, they are fine, but a Waynesville Police Detective and a Juvenile Officer are at Stephanie's house right now, talking to Stephanie and Roger."

I hung up the phone and rushed from the Chief's office into the hallway, where Sgt. Green was waiting for me. He said, "I already know what's going on. Just go. I'll grab your gear from your cruiser and put it in my office."

Everyone knew how close Raymond, Clara, Carol and I were, and how I felt about their children, Roger and Stephanie. I had even brought them to police department social functions. Most of the officers knew their names and considered them friends too.

Sgt. Green only had to say that once, and I left. I made the twenty-minute drive to my house in just under ten minutes. When I got home, there were two unmarked police cars parked in the Longways' driveway. I went into my house and saw Annie sitting on the couch in the living room. She looked like she had been crying.

The minute Annie saw me, she started crying, and said, "It wasn't Stephanie's fault, Daddy." She hopped off the couch, ran into my extended arms, and buried her little face in my neck, with her head on my shoulder. I said, "I know honey. I'm sorry that this happened to Stephanie. It's not her fault. Are you okay?" Annie said, "Yes."

The police officers came over and asked to speak with Annie while I was trying to comfort her. I excused myself, carried Annie into her bedroom, closing the door behind us, and I sat down on the bed, with her still clinging tightly to me. I felt terrible. Stephanie and Annie were so close. She was at our house all the time, and when she wasn't, Annie would be at Stephanie's. I was angry and sad that this had happened. My first impulse was to say, "See. I told you so," but I knew that that would only cause greater division and hurt people's feelings. I never did say it, but I did think it.

Annie was so sad that it made me sad. When Annie saw tears streaming down my face, she said, "Don't cry, Daddy. I'm okay, and Stephanie will be after the police leave." I just hugged her tightly and rocked back and forth. I dried my eyes, and then Annie told me what that "Bad boy Arthur" had done to her friend Stephanie. I asked her if Arthur had done anything to her, and she said, "No, just to Stephanie. It happened at Stephanie's house, last night."

Arthur was arrested and charged as an adult. The story made the local news and after several court appearances and a trial by judge, Arthur Wescott was found guilty of sexually molesting Stephanie, and was sentenced to incarceration of 2-4 years, with four years of probation after his release.

Chief Whitmore and Sgt. Green were extremely supportive throughout that ordeal. They knew what good friends Annie and Stephanie were, and how I had been affected by this hitting so close to home. After struggling for some time with all of this, I found that I couldn't move past it until I managed to tuck it in my private secret compartment deep in the recesses of my mind, and then I could move on.

Life has taught me that sometimes bad things happen to good people. We can't control what happens to us, or our friends and family, but we can control how we choose to deal with it.

For a long time, Chief Whitmore and Sgt. Green checked on me and asked about Annie and her friend Stephanie every few weeks, to make sure that we were all dealing with all of the stress and emotions of the event. But about a year ago, they had stopped asking, and I was good with that. I did not want to dwell on the past. I didn't want to be defined by one thing in my life, and I certainly didn't want Annie and Stephanie to be defined by Arthur's actions either.

I believed then and still do, to this day, that Sgt. Green's checking on me when he first arrived on the scene was an act of kindness and compassion. He was not suggesting that I was not up to performing my job, but following through, with one more check on me, not so unlike what he and the Chief had done in the weeks following the incident with Stephanie.

Annie and Stephanie, who were probably stronger than me all along, never dwelled on what happened. I think they actually got over it long before Raymond, Clara, Carol, or I did. The subject came up once, when Annie was in her teens, and we openly discussed it, but we all chose to leave it in the past. Annie and Stephanie put it behind them and moved on. They ultimately grew up to become very strong, self-confident, young women, who I am very proud of. Annie and Stephanie remain good friends to this day.

5

WHEN ADDITIONAL OFFICERS ARRIVED AT THE PARK, WE SECURED the crime scene and began methodically searching every square inch of it. We were looking for anything that might shed some light on what had happened here, and who may have been responsible for it. It would be virtually impossible to commit a crime of this nature and not have left behind some hair, fiber, trace or serological evidence. We were also looking for possible witnesses, or individuals who may have been in the park earlier and seen something, or someone, even if they did not realize that what they had seen might be important. Twelve police officers spent four hours searching for evidence and possible witnesses in the park.

Johnson Street Park was a picturesque New England community playground and recreational park with two large community swimming pools, bordered by four pavilion buildings, several ball fields and tennis courts, three basketball courts along the east end and center of the park, a bicycle track and skate park and nature trails that ran through a large woodlot along the south side, which was also the railroad track side of the park. The park was on thirty-eight premium acres of real estate in the Waterford Village. This was created as a safe place for kids to play.

How could something like this happen here? The park was utilized by more than twenty thousand visitors annually. Once the winter snow melted, there could be as many as one hundred people in the park at any given time on any single day. That number increased proportionately as temperatures warmed and summer approached. At its peak, with the municipal swimming pool opened up, as many as two thousand people could be in the park at any given time.

Within two hours of starting the search of the park, our efforts paid off. At approximately 6:30 pm, I located two witnesses, who were park employees. They had been working near the ball fields in the southeast corner of the park earlier today.

The rain had continued all afternoon and I was soaked to the bone, as were they. But the rain did not appear to be letting up, so we ducked under the cover of the roof overhanging from one of the park pavilion structures, to get out of the rain and talk. The oldest of the two men identified himself as Mike Whitley, and said he was a Parks and Recreation Foreman, for Waterford Village. The second man identified himself as Walter Kid, adding that he was a Village Parks and Recreation employee, working under Mike's supervision. He described himself as a jack-of-all-trades.

Mike said that he and Walter had both seen two strangers in the park earlier today. They said that they thought that the two strangers were in the park between 3 and 4 pm this afternoon. The two men they described were on foot, and had disappeared into the woods after hanging around the tennis courts for a short time. Mike and Walter said that the tennis courts were right in front of the footpath that cuts through the woods and leads to the railroad tracks at the back of the park.

Both men, independent of one another, said that they had seen the same two men here yesterday as well. They thought that they had seen them here around the same time too—between 3 and 4 pm.

I separated them and had each of them provide descriptions of the two males that they had seen. I didn't want them to hear each other's descriptions, because sometimes, one witness can be influenced by the other, and will change what they might say in order to sound more like what they heard the other person say.

From their separate descriptions, I learned that one of the men was tall, approximately six foot, with a slim build, and an acne-speckled face. He was estimated to be in his mid to early twenties, with wavy, wiry, bushy blonde hair. He was wearing blue jeans, and a long-sleeved, light-colored, button-up shirt. He also had on blue sneakers with yellow stripes.

The second man was heavier, with dark hair, and a full, closely cropped beard. He was estimated to be five foot eight to five foot ten, and weighed between one-hundred-eighty-five and two-hundred pounds. His hair was straight and black. He was wearing a plaid, wool, hunting shirt and a red baseball cap. Mike and Walter both said that the dark-haired male appeared to be older than the blonde-haired male they had each described.

As I wrapped up my interviews with Mike and Walter, I was pleased that the information they had provided would help us to identify the bastards who had done this. Someone else must have seen them here as well—especially if they were here on two different days, back-to-back. Maybe once we were able to get the news about this crime out and the suspects' descriptions, people who may have been in the area, or seen something would call the Waterford Police Station with their information, and we would start collecting additional details about the suspects.

Mike and Walter's statements made me start to think that the suspects may have scouted the park the day before they committed their planned crime. They may have been scouting for their potential victims because yesterday and today were both school days, and the kids who cut through the park every day would have used that path on both days. Suspects who commit crimes like this tend to be predatory. They often scout their prey, or victims before they carry out their crimes. It's been documented time and again.

I was still in the park later that evening, when a young boy, maybe eight or nine years old, came up to me and asked if something bad had happened in the park today. I said that there had been an incident that had occurred here a little earlier, this afternoon. He asked me if I could tell him what had happened because he was looking for his elder sister, and he couldn't find her anywhere. He said that she always came home right after school and today she had not.

He said that his name was Billy Whitcomb, and his elder sister's name was Stacie Whitcomb. "Oh my God," I thought, "Wendy had said her friend's name was Stacie." Billy then described his sister and his sister's best friend Wendy Redding to me. He said that they always walked home together because they lived just down the street from one another.

Billy said that Stacie and Wendy always cut through the park to the railroad tracks on their way home. He said it was a shortcut, and that all the kids from the south side of the village did this as well. He said that once through the woods, they walked down the tracks to Park Street, which is a short distance from Depot Street, where they both lived. Billy said that Stacie and Wendy went to school right across the street from the park, as he turned and pointed towards Johnson Street Elementary School.

I felt like I had been punched in the stomach as Billy continued inquiring and talking about his missing sister. I knew what he did not. The dead girl under the mattress in the woods was Stacie Whitcomb—Billy's missing, elder sister, and her friend, Wendy Redding, who had been rushed to the hospital with life-threatening injuries, was the survivor of this attack.

Billy said that while he was looking for his sister, he had come across some boys that he goes to school with, near the Five Corners intersection, located in the middle of Waterford Village, and that they had told him to check over at Johnson Street Park because the police were over there, and something very bad had happened there earlier today.

I told Billy that I couldn't talk to him about it right now, but that I was going to get someone over here, who could help him with his search for his sister. I then contacted Detective Sgt. Green, stepped a few feet away from Billy, with my back turned to him, so that I could tell Sgt. Green as quietly as possible about Billy's information and inquiries. Sgt. Green immediately stopped what he was doing and came to my location to meet with Billy. After speaking with Billy for only a few minutes, Detective Green drove the young man back to the police station.

My heart broke for the boy—this nightmare was just beginning to unfold for him and his family... A nightmare so horrific that the entire state of Vermont would be repulsed by the details and gravity of it. Our small, crimeless community would be changed forever.

From history and actual life experiences, we have all learned that a crime like this affects many more people than just the immediate family of the crime victim and their loved ones. Not that I am trying to minimize the loss or impact experienced by the Whitcomb and Redding families and the many friends of the girls, or the friends of the two respective families... However, it needs to be said that all of the police, fire, and rescue personnel, who had any involvement in this case or were involved in this criminal investigation in any way would be deeply affected by this incident, and that it would follow them for the rest of their lives.

The list of individuals impacted by this crime begins with the victims and their friends and families. But the emergency responders and the prosecutors, medical examiner, local churches, the Waterford funeral director, municipal officials in the village and town, and court personnel, were all emotionally impacted by this despicable crime. Every single person exposed to a crime like this is affected—each in different ways and for different reasons. It would take years for all of those individuals and this community to fully recover from today's tragic events. Some of those touched by this crime would eventually move on but would live with those memories for the rest of their lives.

Before Billy showed up at the Johnson Street Park, we were not completely satisfied that our dead victim was, in fact, Stacie Whitcomb. However, based on the description that Billy had provided and the details about Stacie and Wendy that Billy had given, we were now feeling confident about saying that the body was that of Stacie Whitcomb, Wendy Redding's schoolmate and best friend. A positive identification, however, would not come until Stacie's father, Joseph Whitcomb, viewed her small, lifeless body at the morgue and confirmed that it was his daughter.

After speaking to Billy at the police station, Sgt. Green learned the names of his parents, and got their contact information, including their telephone numbers, and their home addresses. Stacie's father's name was Joseph Whitcomb, and her mother's name was Sally Whitcomb. Sgt. Green learned that Joseph Whitcomb was a local businessman, who owned the Village Hardware Store on East Street.

Armed with this information, Sgt. Green made contact with Stacie's father, Joseph, and arranged to meet with him and his family at their home in Waterford Village, in thirty minutes.

The Whitcomb home was within a mile of this grizzly crime scene. Their home was a typical wooden framed raised ranch, built in the '60s, on one of many side streets in this area of Waterford Village. Sgt. Green had verified and confirmed everything that Billy had said regarding his sister Stacie and her friend Wendy through Billy's mother and father Joseph and Sally Whitcomb.

The Whitcombs said that Stacie and Wendy were inseparable, and that they walked to and from school together every day, and had done so since the second grade. Sally said that the duo had recently decided to go into the babysitting business together. Sally showed Sgt. Green one of the many hand-made posters that Stacie and Wendy had made and distributed throughout the neighborhood.

Before leaving the park that evening, I recalled seeing the older, white-haired gentleman, standing right where I had asked him to, wearing a yellow rain slicker. He had a look of genuine concern and sadness on his face. He looked like a storybook version of anyone and everyone's grandfather—not overdressed, but well-dressed. An unassuming figure doing what he was doing with no fanfare or notoriety.

When I was relieved from the crime scene and returned to the police station, I made a quick telephone call home, to Carol, my wife, and told her to lock the doors and keep the kids within sight. Carol said that she had seen a breaking news trailer on the television, late this afternoon, saying that there had been a murder in one of the parks, in Waterford Village today—the trailer promised that the full story would be revealed on the late-night news.

Carol asked what had happened, and I told her that I couldn't talk about it right now, but that I would explain everything when I got home later.

It was hard for me to talk about it without getting a lump in my throat. She asked if I was okay, and I said, "Yes."

I wouldn't know it for several years, but many of the other officers had also called home. After all, this was Vermont. Horrendous crimes like this just didn't happen here, or at least they hadn't until today. Many Vermont residents never even locked the doors to their homes at night, or when they went on vacation back then, and probably still don't to this day.

6

At 9:30 pm, Detective Sergeant Bob Green called all of the police units who were on the road into the station. He then gathered all of the officers working on this case into the general police meeting and training room, along with the called-in road officers, and announced that we were having a briefing and an update on this case. He wanted to make sure that we all had the most recent and most complete information available, about today's attack and murder at the Johnson Street Park.

Neary County State's Attorney Jack Banfield and Sgt. Green conducted the evening's briefing. Sgt. Green started by describing the call to the Waterford Police Station at 4:30 pm, this afternoon. He then described everything that Officers Killen, Jones, and I had done, and the work we were continuing to do. Together, Sgt. Green and State's Attorney Banfield spoke about the information provided by the two witnesses that I had found and interviewed near the baseball fields at the park this evening, and he shared the descriptions that Mike and Walter had provided me with of the two possible suspects that they had described seeing in the park.

They talked about Billy Whitcomb showing up at the park, and the information that he had provided that led to the identification of Stacie, Billy's elder sister, as the deceased victim in the park. They spoke briefly about the meeting and notification of Stacie's parents regarding the death of their daughter.

Sgt. Green said that the surviving victim, Wendy Redding, was in very bad shape and presently in the intensive care unit of the local hospital. Green said that Wendy was in critical condition. He added that the hospital prognosis was that if Wendy was strong enough, she could survive her injuries. However, she was very weak at this time, and her condition could either improve or worsen overnight.

Sgt. Green said that he had learned that the two girls were each twelve years old and that both were believed to have been left for dead by their assailants after the attack. According to Sgt. Green, Wendy had said that when she regained consciousness, she had laid very still on the ground, under the mattress that she had been covered with until she was certain that the killers were gone and had left the area.

Green said that Wendy then climbed out from under the mattress and started walking to try and find someone to help her. Sgt. Green said that some of Wendy's details were still a little vague at this time, but the physicians treating her at the hospital attributed her unclear memory to the fact that Wendy was in shock immediately after the attack, and was still in shock when she arrived at the hospital emergency room. The physicians said that as Wendy's medical condition improved, her memory should improve as well.

A train conductor named Henry Thompson was in the caboose of a passing train when he spotted Wendy stumbling from the footpath in the woods onto the railroad tracks. Mr. Thompson said that he called the train engineer on his portable radio, as he hopped off the train and ran to the little girl's aid. Henry Thompson, the train conductor, was the man that I had seen helping Wendy when I had initially arrived on Elm Street, with officers Killen and Jones, earlier this afternoon.

The hospital had confirmed that Wendy's throat had been slit several times, and that she had been stabbed in the chest repeatedly. One of those stab wounds had punctured her left lung. Hospital physicians had also found that she had been shot with a pellet gun, in the back of the head, and between her shoulder blades. Both pellets were deeply embedded in Wendy's skin, suggesting that they were more powerful than the average, run-of-the-mill pellet guns available at most big-box stores in the region, or that the gun was held very close to Wendy, when it was fired.

The Emergency Room physicians had told police that the stab wounds to Wendy's chest had barely missed her heart, and that the cuts to her throat were not deep enough to sever her carotid artery on either side of her neck. They speculated that Wendy had survived because of those two factors. Sgt. Green told us that Wendy was under police guard at this time. He and State's Attorney Banfield shared their concern that when the attackers learned that one of the girls had survived, they might try to find Wendy and kill her, to eliminate any witness to their crime—as that appeared to have been their original intent after the assaults.

After having been provided with that information by Sgt. Green, officers speculated that Stacie Whitcomb was not as fortunate as Wendy, and that her attacker, unlike Wendy's, was more violent, and had inflicted fatal injuries to Stacie, following the assault. We would not know that for certain until after the autopsy, which would be conducted tomorrow morning, at 10 am.

The briefing ended with Sgt. Green telling us that no murder weapon(s), or guns for that matter, had been recovered at, or near the crime scene, so there was a possibility that the two attackers had taken them after they committed their crime(s).

As the meeting broke up, we were all directed to be back in for a 9 am briefing tomorrow morning. Tomorrow's briefing would be much of what we had just been told, coupled with any new information learned overnight, but it would be a larger meeting that would include other area detectives and police officers, who would be joining us in our investigation. Those other officers would be on loan to us from other police agencies in the county and the Vermont State Police. They would specifically be here to help out with this major case. Their assignments to our agency would be for as long as we needed them.

I was filled with anxiety. I found myself thinking that rather than going home, we should all get back out there and try to find the girl's attackers. Having never really been involved in a major investigation of this magnitude,

I had not yet learned the lessons of preserving your human resources for the longer haul and multi-tasking police operations and assignments.

First things first, however. It was late and everyone was soaking wet, hungry, and tired. It was a pitch-black night with no stars in the sky. We would have to break for the night and begin afresh in the morning.

7

As I drove home from work, I could not get the images of the girls out of my mind. I must have relived the entire incident in my head a dozen times during that drive—thinking about my daughter and how close to Wendy and Stacie's age and size she was.

With each image flashing through my mind, I couldn't help thinking about how scared the girls must have been when they were being attacked and sexually assaulted. These were little girls. What kind of animals would do this sort of thing?

When I arrived home, I could not even recall driving my car there. I had driven to get there I was certain, but I was so preoccupied with thoughts about the crime scene, the girls, and of course, the killers that I just couldn't recall the drive home. It was almost as though my total concentration was on Wendy and Stacie, and anything else that I did, I was doing automatically.

The first thing I did when I got into the house was to peek into the kids' bedroom and look at my sleeping children. My mind would not stop racing with the events of the day. I had a huge lump in my throat that I could barely swallow, but somehow, did. I fought back tears as I kissed Jared and Annie on their foreheads lightly, so as not to wake them up. As I gazed at their innocent faces, I fought the urge to just break down.

I needed to be strong. I needed to keep those sad and angry feelings bottled up inside of me—converting all that negative energy into positive energy that would empower me with drive and determination, making sure that we do not allow anything to sidetrack us, or delay our finding the individuals who did this, and bringing them to justice.

We must catch the people who did this horrible thing, and we had to catch them sooner, rather than later. A sense of fear that a repeat of today's incident could or would happen kept every police officer in Neary County and the entire state of Vermont on pins and needles. No one would rest until the Johnson Street Park attack was solved and the suspects were behind bars.

Carol wanted to talk about what had happened in the park, but I didn't feel very chatty. I gave her the fifty words or less, thumbnail sketch of what had happened and then went to bed for the night. I was exhausted, and I had to get some rest for tomorrow, and make sure I wasn't late for the briefing in the morning.

Try as I might, I could not sleep. My mind was overstimulated. Thoughts about the day's events and what tomorrow would bring were bouncing around in my mind. Thoughts about how to proceed with the investigation, what we should do first etc., coursed through my mind. I continued to think about the girls and the ferocious nature of this attack. Together, all of these thoughts kept me awake most of the night.

I tossed and turned as I watched each hour pass on the digital alarm clock to my right, on the nightstand. I watched that clock all through the night. With each passing hour, I stressed a little more about how I needed to get some sleep, or I would be exhausted all day tomorrow. By morning, I was frustrated that I hadn't slept and found myself rolling out of bed feeling just as tired as I was when I went to bed, barely sleeping a wink.

Once I was out of bed in the morning, I immediately started thinking about the girls, and I started contemplating the crime scene in my head over and over again, while I shaved and showered. I was wondering what clue, if any, may have been missed or overlooked. Was there something here that we failed to see or pick up on?

I tried to shake it off, but with no real success. I knew that I would have the images of those girls in my mind for the rest of my life. I would take Wendy and Stacie with me everywhere I went. That would likely not change regardless of whether or not this crime was ever solved. Stacie deserved to be remembered. At least I would never forget Stacie and the tragic and sudden end of her young life. Even thinking about her now, I can feel my breathing quicken and my heart rate increase.

I was changed forever. Any hint of innocence or naïveté that I ever had regarding just how cruel one human being could be to another, was gone. I refused to allow that train of thought to pervade my persona and stop me from being a relatively happy person, but knowing and understanding that basic principle served me well, as I continued in my chosen career path. I find it troubling, but I now understand that people can do unimaginable things to one another. I would never feel the same way about a cool, spring rain again, and my comfort level with public parks and outdoor spaces in Vermont would never be what it was before the Johnson Street Park incident again.

At some point in every police officer's career, they will become suspicious of strangers, the stories they tell, and the unfolding events that find their way into the officer's presence, whether on duty or off. It takes a little longer for some police officers to develop that police instinct or cop cynicism, especially in a state like Vermont, where the sheer volume of crime and the violent nature of it is so much less than in those large, metropolitan areas of the country. The instinct to become suspicious of strangers' kicks into gear for some officers mostly because of the frequency with which those officers deal with serious and major crimes. It begins for them when they leave the police academy and start training in a squad car on the streets. While this instinct comes to everyone who wears a badge and carries a gun, it just happens much quicker to some, than others. And as it develops in most officers, it causes them to be more cautious and suspicious of everyone, all the time. With this attack on Wendy and Stacie in Johnson Street Park, it had now started happening with me.

I would no longer sit in a restaurant with my back to the door, or not be fully cognizant of my surroundings and the people around me all the time, or ever alert to the people that I passed on the street, or saw on the biking trail or at the local playground and so forth. I once believed that all people were generally good, and only a small percentage was bad. I now believed that there is an equal ratio of good and bad people in this world, and until someone could prove to me that they were good, I withheld any opinion, one way or the other.

To this very day, when I find myself outside, in a spring rain, my thoughts immediately go back to May 15, 1981, and I remember Wendy Redding and Stacie Whitcomb. I often wonder what has become of Wendy, and I wonder how she's doing. Is she married? Does she have children of her own? What's she like? How does she cope with what happened to her and her friend? I also think about Stacie Whitcomb. I wonder what she would be like today if she had not been murdered in the park. How her life would have turned out... Whether or not she would still live in Waterford, Vermont... I wonder what she might have done with her life. Would she and Wendy still be best friends? Would she be married and would her father have given her away at her wedding ceremony?

I will never forget Stacie Whitcomb and how sad it makes me feel to think about her lost innocent life. She will always be twelve years old in my mind. As I am transposing my long-held secret thoughts to written words, I have goosebumps running up and down my arms, and that all too familiar lump in my throat reemerges.

The news stories and headlines that followed Stacie and Wendy's attack in Vermont newspapers and on the local television broadcasts were quickly picked up by television stations across the country, and the Johnson Street Park attack became national headline news. Every major television station across the entire United States led with the story on May 16, 1981. Everyone who heard about this case was captivated and aghast at the same time as they learned the age of the victims, the nature of the attack, and the gruesome details of the girl's torture, rape, and murder, and in Wendy's case, attempted murder.

Our small, rural community had made national news and we were in disbelief. Vermonters are proud of their state. They are proud to be known for lush, green mountains, pristine brooks and waterways, rural landscapes, four seasons, and for Vermont maple syrup, but not for a violent, unimaginable crime. The Johnson Street Park attack would be permanently seared in the minds of most Vermonters, and would be a blemish on Vermont's long-standing, peaceful, and mostly boring history.

8

When I showed up for the briefing the next morning, there were at least twenty-eight officers and detectives from several area police agencies and the Vermont State Police already present, and more would trickle in over the next hour. That number didn't even include the Waterford Police Department's nineteen officers, who were all there as well.

There were FBI and ATF agents, U.S. Marshals, and Border Patrol Officers in attendance as well as several Neary County Deputy State's Attorneys and a host of municipal and state police officers, and detectives from the other departments in our region. They were all assigned to this investigation by their respective agencies for as long as need be.

I stopped trying to count them when the number reached fifty-three. This was a law enforcement community that came together to help one another when needed. No one was going to get away with this in our small, peaceful community or our state.

At the briefing, which was once again conducted by State's Attorney Banfield and Detective Sgt. Green, we started by standing and introducing ourselves, one at a time. When that was done, they told us that one of the Waterford Police Department's midnight-shift officers, Cpl. Lance Buckman, had gone back over to the Johnson Street Park. Armed with his flashlight, he had conducted his own cursory search of the park looking for any possible evidence or weapons that may have been discarded by the suspects on their way out of the park, which may have been overlooked or missed by the search officers earlier.

At 3:20 am, Cpl. Buckman had found and photographed a wooden-handled, serrated-edged cutting blade, steak knife in the tree line, several hundred feet from the crime scene. The tree line where he found the knife was directly behind the tennis courts, on the west side of the front of Johnson Street Park. The knife had blood on its blade and was lying on top of the recently mowed grass. It was photographed and seized, and Cpl. Buckman was driving it to the Vermont State Police, Crime Laboratory right now, even as the rest of us were meeting here at the station. Sgt. Green then told us that Wendy's condition had improved during the night, and that early this morning, she had provided a much more detailed statement and descriptions of both assailants.

Some of the information that would follow at this morning's briefing was the same as we had heard last night, but it was good to hear it again and I made several notes. The senior officers managing this major case wanted all of the newly assigned officers in the room to have the same information.

Sgt. Green continued, "Wendy said that there were two males. One was younger in appearance and acted younger than the other. The older male had dark hair while the younger one had blonde hair. The dark-haired male was more dominant and seemed to be in charge. He was also the more aggressive and more violent of the two of them."

Both suspects were armed with pistols (that would turn out to be pellet handguns), and each had a wooden-handled kitchen knife, similar in description to the one found by Cpl. Buckman in the tree line at Johnson Street Park last night.

The suspects waited in the bushes along the footpath, near the cross-cut path closest to the railroad tracks until the girls got very close to their position. As the girls came near, they both jumped from their hiding places, and with their guns pointed at each of them, the suspects ordered the girls into the woods.

Wendy said that they were forced to walk deeper into the woods until they reached the clearing—where Stacie's body was eventually found—and then they were attacked. Wendy added that there were two dirty, foam mattresses, on opposite sides of the clearing, almost as if they had been staged and put there. She went on to describe discarded trash and empty soda and beer bottles strewn around the clearing as well.

The dark-haired man dragged Stacie to one of the foam mattresses in the clearing, and the younger, blonde man dragged Wendy to the other foam mattress on the other side of the clearing. When the dark-haired suspect opened his fly and exposed his penis, ordering Stacie to touch it, she balked at his orders. The dark-haired man promptly shot her with his gun in her right eye.

When Stacie cried out on being shot, the dark-haired man shot her two more times—this time in the throat.

At this point, the two suspects each took one of Stacie and Wendy's knee socks, and tied it around their heads and through the girls' mouths so that they couldn't cry out or scream anymore. To avoid being shot again, Stacie did what the suspect ordered her to do. And having just seen the consequences of Stacie's refusal to do what she was told to do, when Wendy was ordered to do the same thing with the younger, blonde-haired suspect, she complied. Before the assault was over, the dark-haired suspect would shoot Stacie again, in her back.

All of this new information was helpful. You could feel a surge of disbelief and recommitted energy growing in the room. We were going to get these bastards. They would not be allowed to get away with such a despicable crime. I would not say that we felt energized—but we did feel driven to find these two scumbags.

A Vermont State Police Detective Sgt., whose reputation as a criminal investigator was unsurpassed, had joined our investigative leadership team. His name was Victor Spano. He brought a larger-than-life attitude about who the good guys were, who the bad guys were, and how we would find the people responsible for committing this crime.

He and I would grow to become good friends later. Sgt. Spano was a "take charge" kind of person with a "no-nonsense" attitude. He was well respected by coworkers, prosecutors, and judges alike. Detective Sgt. Spano was a celebrated criminal investigator, whose reputation preceded him. Before completing his career with the Vermont State Police, Sgt. Spano would work his way up through the rank and file, finally, retiring as a Major, in charge of the State Police Criminal Division in the late '90s.

As the investigation proceeded, Sgt. Spano would prove to be the person that the rest of us looked to for direction and guidance. He was not the highest-ranking person in the room, but he was the person that commanded everyone's attention and respect, whom everyone gladly took orders from—even those who outranked him.

Sgt. Spano and Sgt. Green shared responsibility of giving everyone their assignments, and everyone reported back to them upon completion of each assignment. My respect and appreciation for Sgt. Spano would grow as we worked this case together and many others in the future. He is a man that I was and still am proud to call a brother officer and my friend.

A second Vermont State Trooper, Sgt. Willy Francis, who had been trained as a criminal sketch artist, was brought in—he was the investigator who had met with Wendy at the hospital earlier this morning. Sgt. Francis had not only obtained a much more detailed account of the attack, but he had also worked with Wendy, and hand-drawn sketches of the two suspects who attacked her and Stacie. Wendy Redding had seen what Sgt. Francis had drawn and had assured him that the sketches of each of the two suspects looked just like the two attackers.

From her hospital bed, Wendy showed great strength and determination, reliving and retelling the horrible story, with all the details of the attack. She also provided detailed descriptions of the two assailants' conduct and behavior throughout the attack. Wendy inspired every one of us to dig deeper and to keep pushing ourselves forward. She was the bravest twelve-year-old girl any of us had ever met or known.

Sgt. Francis' sketches were distributed among all of the police officers and detectives at the briefing and sent to the other Neary County police agencies in the area. They would eventually be more broadly distributed to all law enforcement agencies across the entire state of Vermont, and by late today they would be distributed to all of the news outlets and reporters following this story as well.

In Wendy's detailed statement, she said that the dark-haired suspect paired off with Stacie, and the blonde male paired off with her. The girls were then forced to take off all of their clothes. During the early stages of the attack, Wendy heard Stacie say, "I'm only twelve years old… This can't be happening in Vermont." That is when Wendy said that Stacie was shot again by the dark-haired male. The two girls were then forcibly raped, Stacie by the dark-haired male and Wendy by the younger blonde-haired male. Both girls were penetrated by their attackers repeatedly. Both anally and vaginally.

Wendy said that while they were being raped, she heard the dark-haired suspect say, "Now you're going to know what it feels like to squeal and be slaughtered like a pig," or words to that effect.

Investigators would later learn that the dark-haired suspect—Tony Hampton—had accompanied his father, Gerald Hampton, to a pig-slaughtering at a relative's farm over the weekend, before the attack.

Wendy described the pain she experienced during the sexual assault as "excruciating" and said that sometime after the blonde-haired male's forced sexual penetration began, she passed out. She couldn't remember anything after that until the moment she awoke under the mattress in the clearing.

When the suspects finished raping the girls, they stabbed them in the chest repeatedly and cut their throats. It was believed and later confirmed during a confession by the blond-haired suspect—John Pitco—that both girls had passed out from the pain they experienced during the assault. Stacie Whitcomb would not survive, while Wendy Redding would regain consciousness and crawl out from under the dirty foam mattress, and seek help.

9

EACH OF THE OFFICERS WORKING ON THIS INVESTIGATION HAD voiced their individual and collective commitment to finding the heartless scumbags that had committed this crime and done these horrible things to Wendy and Stacie.

Wendy was never far from any of our thoughts. As she lay in her hospital bed fighting to recover from her life-threatening injuries, a collection was taken up by the officers working the case and a large stuffed teddy bear was purchased with the donated money. The bear was then brought to a local seamstress, who sewed a police patch from each law enforcement agency that had police officers working on the case, onto that bear. When the stuffed teddy bear was finished, it was presented to Wendy with a 'get well' card, signed by each one of us.

An autopsy was performed on Stacie Whitcomb on May 16, by the Chief Medical Examiner Dr. Andrea Lewis. Dr. Lewis had confirmed that there were two pellets lodged in the back of Stacie's neck, near her spine, one in her lower back and one in her right eye. Dr. Lewis said that the two pellets in Stacie's throat had entered the front of her throat and traveled through her neck to the back of her neck, where they came to rest, near her spine.

Stacie had also sustained four separate stab injuries to her chest—one of them directly to Stacie's heart, which she ruled had caused almost immediate death. The Medical Examiner recovered semen, pubic hair, and trace fiber evidence from Stacie's body as well.

Dr. Lewis reviewed Wendy Redding's medical records and concluded that Stacie and Wendy had sustained almost identical injuries during the attack, but Wendy's attacker had failed to inflict any fatal injuries to his victim. She summarized that in her professional opinion, Wendy's non-lethal injuries were meant to kill her, but the blonde-haired suspect's inflicted injuries were *accidentally* non-lethal.

Dr. Lewis further summarized that the younger, blonde-haired suspect, who by all accounts had the weaker personality of the two assailants, had inflicted injuries to Wendy that were the result of him copying everything that the dark-haired suspect had done to Stacie.

Finally, Dr. Lewis summarized that the assailants had left both girls for dead, following the attack.

Once Wendy Redding started to recover, no one was more determined than she was to help catch the two suspects responsible for Stacie's murder and her own savage rape, torture, and attempted murder.

At a briefing later in the day on May 16, 1981, we learned that a caller had described seeing a suspicious vehicle and two suspicious male occupants in it, who had parked near the caller's home on a cul-de-sac in the neighboring community of Middleton Falls late on the night of the Johnson Street Park attack. The caller described an overheard conversation that sounded like it might be related to this crime.

Two officers, Officer Pete Fairway and Officer Donald Sands, were dispatched to the caller's home to follow up on this information. even while the rest of us were being updated and briefed. Approximately halfway through the second briefing, Sgt. Spano said that the assigned officers who had followed up on that call had just spoken with him by telephone and reported that when they interviewed the female caller, Tracey Wells, she and her husband, James Wells had both said that they had seen and overheard the same thing.

Tracey said that there were two suspicious men in a blue, older model, Chevrolet station wagon. They had parked in the cul-de-sac, directly in front of their home, and turned the vehicle off. She said that she and James overheard the two men talking about what they would say if questioned by the police about the Johnson Street Park incident. She reported that they had agreed to say that they were both in Banbury, at one of their houses, if asked.

Tracey said that the two men didn't discuss the incident more specifically, and neither her husband nor she could see the men well enough to describe them. She estimated that they might be in their early twenties. She said that she made that estimate based solely on the sound of their voices as neither she nor her husband ever actually saw their faces. However, they were able to say with some degree of certainty that there were two occupants in the vehicle and they were both male.

I felt like this may be a solid lead. Immediately following the briefing, I spoke with Sgt. Spano about a news story that I had seen on the nightly news a while ago, regarding the solving of the New York City Police Department's serial murder investigation that led to the NYPD detectives identifying and arresting David Richard Berkowitz, better known as the Son of Sam and the .44 Caliber Killer, in New York City.

I explained that in that investigation, detectives had checked NYPD's parking tickets and found the registered owner of one of the parking violation vehicles to be one of their persons of interest in their serial murder investigation. The registered owner of that vehicle was David Richard Berkowitz, who would later be arrested, criminally charged, and convicted for several of the murders.

Berkowitz's vehicle had been parked illegally in the area of one of the more recent killings in New York City, and a Parking Enforcement Officer had issued the vehicle a parking ticket for being illegally parked.

I told him that I wanted to follow up on Tracey and James Well's phone call and the information that they had provided about the two suspicious men in the blue Chevrolet station wagon on the night of the attack, by trying the same thing that NYPD had done. I told him that I was willing to try anything if it would move our investigation forward. Both, Sgt. Spano and Sgt. Green thought that it was worth a shot, and assigned me to go ahead and do that.

Fully aware that the Waterford Police Department was a much smaller police agency than the New York City Police Department, I didn't only check just parking tickets, but also checked all of our most recent, combined parking and traffic offense tickets.

After skimming through three-hundred and sixteen traffic and parking tickets issued in the past two months, I found that one of our officers, Harley Jacob, had issued a traffic ticket for defective equipment, to an older, two-toned (dark blue lower half and lighter colored blue roof), four-door Pontiac with a loud muffler and the left headlight out, just one month ago. The vehicle was being operated at that time by John Pitco, a well-known male juvenile delinquent, who lived with his parents at 5 Wiley Lane, here in the Waterford Village. The vehicle was registered to his mother, Louise Pitco. Most of the Waterford Police Department's officers knew or had firsthand experience with John Pitco and all of his dysfunctional family members.

Upon comparing a juvenile record file photo of John Pitco, we quickly discovered that he looked a lot like one of the suspects described by Wendy Redding in the attack. The more we looked at the sketch of the tall, slimmer, younger male, the more convinced we all became that Pitco could very well be the younger of the two suspects we were looking for.

The reasons for the Waterford Police Officer's frequent visits to the Pitco residence ranged in nature from domestic disturbances, to young family members being involved in thefts, vandalism, snowball throwing at passing motor vehicles, to disorderly conduct and physical fights between various family members.

The Pitco family lived just around the corner from the murder scene. There were several children in the family, but the ones that I was most familiar with were the males: Wayne, John, John's older brother, Randy, and their father, Harold.

Two years ago, Randy Pitco had worked as an informant of mine. He had helped me to solve a burglary and recover five-thousand-dollars' worth of stolen property after I had arrested him for driving while his license was under suspension. Randy was a memorable character. When I arrested him on that occasion, he was quick to point out that his driver's license could not be under suspension, because he had never had a Vermont driver's license, to begin with. It was a point that was technically correct—he had never had a Vermont driver's license; he simply drove without one!

I had to explain to him that whether he ever had a driver's license or not, was irrelevant because under Vermont Law, his privilege to operate a motor vehicle, on a public highway in the state of Vermont was suspended. I recall telling him that he had probably received an unpaid traffic ticket, or he had been arrested for operating under suspension on a previous occasion, which would have led to his license being suspended by the Vermont Department of Motor Vehicles. Randy admitted that he had been arrested on a previous occasion for operating under suspension. Additionally, Randy said that he was issued a traffic ticket for speeding on that occasion as well, but that he had never paid it. The long and the short of it was that he negotiated a deal—authorized by the Neary County State's Attorney's Office—to help me recover the stolen property from the burglaries in exchange for a dismissal of his latest driving under suspension charge. I found Randy easy enough to work with, but he was certainly not the brightest bulb in the lamp, if you know what I mean.

I had once chased Randy's younger brother, John Pitco, down Main Street because he was roller-skating in the middle of the road and would not get off the road, or stop, even when I had my emergency lights on and commanded him to stop over my mobile PA system. He had traffic backed up Main Street to the center of town. Cars were blowing their horns and angry motorists were yelling at him through their open car windows. When I finally managed to get him stopped and out of the roadway, he tried to argue with me that he was on wheels—just like all the cars—so he too should be allowed to be on the road.

John always acted goofy, and he often had a wiseass smirk on his face. Whenever you tried to talk to John, he laughed or snickered constantly. I believed that it was sometimes about his stupid antics, and other times, it may have simply been a nervous laugh. He was never violent or aggressive towards me, but was always a handful. I never trusted him, so I never gave him an opportunity to try anything physical with me. John was a smart mouth though, and he would challenge or dispute what he had been stopped for or that what he had done was wrong or illegal. I would characterize him as more rebellious and defiant than aggressive or violent. I recalled John and his brother Randy, getting in a fistfight in the lobby of the Waterford High School—it took the Principal of the school, myself and one other police officer to break them up. Both John and his brother Randy were scrappers, and neither one of them would give up and let the other think that they had won the fight. Even when the fight was over, they still had to be physically restrained and separated.

John had recently started hanging around with an older looking, dark-haired male named Tony Hampton. Tony was from the neighboring community of Banbury. I had spoken to John and Tony on more than one occasion while I was on duty over the last month. On the occasions when I had spoken to Tony, he was always polite and respectful. More so than John Pitco. I would often see the two of them walking the streets at night.

The reason that we had not zeroed in on John Pitco and Tony Hampton as suspects much earlier in this investigation was that Wendy had described the attackers as "being older… in their twenties, with older sounding voices." We would later discover that Wendy's confusion about the possible age of the suspects was due in part to the dark-haired suspect's facial hair and the fact that she felt that his ball cap had made him look older. When you couple those factors with the sexual nature and violence of the attack on the girls, it is fairly easy to understand Wendy's confusion about the possible age of the two suspects.

I think that the police and the criminal investigators were also focused on finding two older male suspects, and did not even consider the possibility of younger male suspects, like Tony Hampton and John Pitco. I know that I had not. Everyone involved in the investigation believed that because of the brutality of the attack, the male suspects would be older. Who could have known?

Now that we had started comparing Tony Hampton and John Pitco to the sketches of our two suspects, we all started to realize how much they resembled the sketches of the two attackers. When we took into consideration John and Tony's knowledge and familiarity of this community and the area in general, where the crime had been committed, the duo looked more and more like our two suspects in this case.

The investigation was starting to take on new energy among the police investigators. We all felt like we were getting closer, and were headed in the right direction. Now we just had to put it all together. There was going to be justice for Wendy and Stacie, and it would come sooner, rather than later.

10

SGT. SPANO TALKED TO ME ABOUT WHETHER I THOUGHT I COULD track Randy Pitco down, and persuade him to help us with our investigation—seeing that I had had a police informant relationship with him in the past when he had worked for me on the burglary and stolen property case. I told him that I thought I could. I also told him that I agreed with his assessment about my past dealings with Randy Pitco, and the fact that he and I already had a good rapport, which improved the possibility that I might find it easier to persuade him to cooperate with us.

Randy may not even realize that any information he could provide us with about his brother, John, and John's friend Tony, could be extremely helpful. You never know, if you never ask.

Sgt. Spano assigned Detective Bill Smart, from a neighboring agency to accompany me. Our joint assignment was to track down Randy Pitco and see what we might learn from him about his younger brother John and Tony. It was a long shot, but everyone agreed that it was worth a try.

I remembered from my earlier dealings with Randy that he spent most of his time at his girlfriend's house, from where I had picked him up on several occasions when he was cooperating on the burglary investigation that we had worked on together. Detective Smart and I drove to Randy's girlfriend's home on the outskirts of Waterford, near the town line between Waterford and Waynesville.

We pulled into his girlfriend's driveway, parked and exited our car. We walked up to the front door and knocked on the door repeatedly. There was no answer and it appeared that no one was at home. I was disappointed and felt a little panicky now. I started thinking, what if they were no longer girlfriend and boyfriend. What if we do find her and she hasn't seen Randy since back around the time that they were together when Randy was working with me. Where do we look now?

I calmed myself down as I reminded myself that this was just the first stop on our mission to find Randy Pitco. I had learned from real-life experience, that even when people separate or breakup, one or the other often still possesses information about their estranged relatives, friends' addresses, telephone numbers, hangouts, etc. Lastly, I thought, we can always try back here again a little later on.

I was racking my brains, trying to think of where else Randy could be as we hopped back in our unmarked police car and started to back out of the driveway. Just as we were backing from the driveway into the road, Randy pulled up, with his directional light on, waiting for us to clear the driveway so that he could pull in. Ahh, we hadn't struck out, after all, I thought.

Randy was alone in the vehicle. What I hadn't even shared with my assigned partner, Detective Smart, yet was that before leaving the police station, I had the Dispatcher check on the status of Randy's driver's license. She had told me that his driving privileges were still actively under suspension.

After backing from the driveway to let Randy pull in, we pulled right back in behind his vehicle. When he parked the car, Detective Smart and I walked right over to his side of the car and he immediately recognized me from our previous dealings. We showed him our badges and IDs anyways, as I introduced Randy to Detective Smart. I told Randy that we had come here looking for him.

Before going any further though, I told him that I knew that his driver's license was still under suspension. After some ridiculous explanation and some half-hearted bantering back and forth with me about how he thought he had "taken care of everything" and he could not be in trouble for driving under suspension if he didn't even know that he was, he stopped. I think even he realized how silly he sounded.

I told him that he was under arrest and that he would need to come back to the police station with us. He moaned, and put his hands behind his back, in a gesture of peaceful surrender. I quickly frisked him, handcuffed him, and put him in the backseat of our car.

Randy was cooperative and repeatedly said that he didn't want any trouble. On the way back to the police station, he told us how well he had been doing and then he tried to negotiate with us and make a deal to get himself out of trouble. After all, it had worked for him on an earlier arrest, involving me. Why not try it again? He asked several times why we had been looking for him to begin with, and I assured him that I would explain everything to him once we got back to the police station.

When we arrived at the station, we moved Randy from the backseat and escorted him into one of the many interview rooms inside. Once settled inside, I removed Randy's handcuffs and told him that we wanted to talk with him about his brother John and John's friend Tony.

Randy was three years older than John, and he seemed to perk up at the idea of providing information about John that he could try to wrangle a deal with us for. The minute I mentioned his brother's name, it was evident from his facial expressions and his exaggerated sigh of relief that he didn't care too much for his brother.

"What do you want to know about John?" he asked. I asked, "What can you tell me about him..." And before he could answer, I followed up with, "... and his friend Tony Hampton?" Randy then started talking about John and Tony. And as he spoke, it became even more evident that Randy didn't like John, but he disliked Tony Hampton even more.

Randy asked, "Is this going to help me out of the driving under suspension charge?" I said, "You know how it works, Randy, if your information is valuable to us, I will talk to the State's Attorney and recommend that he consider dismissing the charges associated with your arrest, but I can't make that deal. Only the State's Attorney can. But he won't if I don't go to bat for you." "Okay," Randy said, and we continued.

Randy told us that John and Tony were together all the time, and that they were very sneaky. He said that they were always whispering to one another. Randy said that he didn't trust either of them and that he had caught the duo in his parent's bedroom, going through their clothes dresser, looking for hidden money.

Randy said that Tony was real bossy, and he would do only whatever he really wanted to do. If he couldn't be in charge, he was not interested. His brother John, on the other hand, was a thief, Randy added, describing the time he had seen John go through his mother's pocketbook and steal money from it. Randy said that when his mother had discovered the missing money and inquired about it, Randy had pointed out John as the culprit. However, John had lied when his mother had confronted him, and denied taking the money. Randy said, "John lies all the time, and for all I know, Tony is a liar and a thief too."

As we were talking, I asked Randy about the kind of things John and Tony would steal. Randy listed some personal items of his own that John had stolen in the past. "John always steals any money that I leave lying on my nightstand. I used to have a small bowl on my nightstand in my bedroom into which I would toss loose change almost every day. But I stopped doing that because John would go through my room and steal the loose change from the bowl," said Randy, adding that when confronted, John would deny doing it.

"I know that John has stolen my parent's car on dozens of occasions, and I know for sure that John stole from my grandparents' garage as well," Randy said, adding, "I saw John steal a chainsaw from the garage at my grandparents' house in Hadley, Vermont. He later bragged to me that he sold it for $200 in Banbury."

After this, Randy launched into a tirade about how he believed that John had stolen his pellet pistol. Randy said over and over again, "I'm pretty sure that John went into my bedroom and stole my pellet gun from under my bed. It was a pellet pistol with a blue barrel that looked just like a real revolver. It had wooden grips and looked like a .357 Magnum revolver."

Randy went on to say that he didn't know why John would steal his pellet gun because John had one of his own, almost identical to Randy's.

Although I never let on at that time, this piece of information was extremely valuable to our investigation because Wendy had said that the attackers were each armed with a gun, that she described "looked like real guns". We also knew from the projectile evidence recovered from the girls' bodies that the guns that had been used to shoot the girls were pellet guns. I felt like this was going very well and I was optimistic about where Randy's information might lead us, but I didn't want to get my hopes up prematurely.

We asked Randy if he had heard about the attack and murder at the Johnson Street Park two days ago. He said that he had heard about it from his friends, and that he had seen a small segment of the news about it. We then showed Randy the sketches of the two male suspects in the Johnson Street Park attack and asked him if he thought that either of the two suspects looked like John and Tony.

Randy looked the sketches over for what seemed like several minutes, and then looked up, to the left side of his head, as if searching his memory. After a minute or two, he nervously said, "Yes. I think that the sketches look just like John and Tony Hampton. Do you think they did this?" he asked. I countered with another question, "More importantly, do you think that they did?"

Randy's response slowed down, and he said with a look of disbelief on his face, "I didn't before you asked me, but now I am thinking yes—I think they did do this. I think those two assholes may very well be the suspects you are looking for." Then, without any solicitation from Detective Smart or me, he said, "If those assholes did this, I hope you throw them in jail for the rest of their lives."

I couldn't help but think that we had just made a giant leap forward in solving this case. As my optimism surged, I carefully controlled myself, so as not to tip my hand about the value of Randy's information.

As we continued to question Randy, he revealed that John had a documented learning disability and was suspected of having Autism Spectrum

Disorder (ASD). However, John's parents, Louise and Harold, would not approve of the school testing him further so that it could be confirmed or ruled out.

Autism Spectrum Disorder is a condition related to brain development that impacts how a person perceives things and socializes with others, causing problems with inappropriate social interaction, behavioral disturbances, unpredictable and irrational behavior, and in some cases, serious deficits in language comprehension and effective communications skills. Once I learned this, I realized that it might explain why John had seemed or acted awkward when I had dealt with him in the past, including his nervous laughter and his tendency to smirk when being talked to.

I asked Randy if he had any recent photographs of John or Tony. He said that he did not have any wallet-sized photos with him, but added, "If I can run over to my house quickly, I might be able to get you a picture of John." Randy lived in his parent's home on Wiley Lane, just two blocks from the police station.

I excused myself from the room and went to speak with Sgt. Green and Sgt. Spano, who immediately brought State's Attorney Banfield into the conversation. After discussing the situation and providing an overview of what Randy had told Detective Smart and me, Banfield asked me if I thought he would return, if he was allowed to leave. I said, "Yes." He then weighed in, and said, "I vote that we let Randy leave the station to go and try to find a photo of John then. Even if Randy doesn't return, we can always get an arrest warrant for him on the DLS (driving while license is suspended) charge." We all agreed.

I went back into the interview room, and told Randy that if I let him run home, he had to promise me that he would come right back. Randy said, "No problem. It will just take me a couple of minutes to get there, find a picture, and get back over here." I asked, "What if John and Tony are at the house?" He said, "Don't worry. I'll just blow them off like I always do." I walked Randy to the back door of the police station, and off he went.

While Randy was gone, Detective Smart and I again reviewed all of the information that Randy had provided us with. We then shared the information with Detective Sgt. Green and Sgt. Spano. They were very interested to hear all of it, and were equally optimistic about how these new developments would play into our unfolding investigation.

Randy Pitco returned to the police station within twenty minutes. He came back with a recent wallet-sized school picture of John, which he gave to us, saying, "I couldn't find any pictures with John and Tony both in them."

We talked a little more, and finally, after Randy agreed to not say anything to anyone about his interactions with the police this afternoon, he was released by the State's Attorney with a promise of a dismissal of his driving under suspension arrest, in exchange for his cooperation in the murder investigation.

11

As it turned out, Randy Pitco would be murdered in St. Andrews, Vermont, in 1984, at the age of twenty. He was murdered by a man named Shane Scully, who according to news reports, had been hired along with Randy, by Gordon Rhodes, a former Vermont legislator, to help carry out a scam to burn down a building in St. Andrews, Vermont' that Rhodes owned, and would collect the property insurance settlement on.

News reports described the three men as local barflies, who thought they were part of the 'movers and shakers' in town. Gordon Rhodes was the youngest person to ever serve in the Vermont Legislature, elected at age 18 in the early 1970s, was the smartest of the trio, and had the most to gain if they were able to pull off their contrived plan to commit insurance fraud.

He was paying Randy and Shane five hundred dollars each for their role in the planned fire. Randy was killed, according to the news report, after Shane and Gordon learned that he had been stopped by the local police and arrested, after leaving a local bar in the early morning hours.

The rumor around town was that Randy had been processed for suspected DWI and for driving while his license was still under suspension. Randy talked too much, to too many people and had bragged about how he had gotten out of trouble on several previous occasions, by negotiating deals with police and prosecutors. Shane and Gordon began thinking that Randy may fall back on his old habits and negotiate with the police once again, to avoid having to go to court on the pending criminal charges.

One night, after making their rounds at the local bars in town, Shane and Gordon convinced Randy to take a ride with them to a remote sandpit, where they wanted to show him something. Having drunk way too much, Randy gladly accompanied them. Near the back of the sandpit, Gordon told Randy that what he wanted to show him was in the trunk of the car, so they exited the vehicle and walked to the rear. As Gordon put the key into the trunk lid, Randy waited in anticipation to see the secret surprise, while Shane quietly positioned himself behind Randy. He never saw Shane pull the pistol from the back of his pants.

Shane slowly raised the weapon to the back of Randy's head and pulled the trigger. Even Gordon jumped when the gun went off. Randy's limp body fell forward, towards the trunk of the car. The autopsy report would later say that Randy Pitco died instantly, from the gunshot to the back of his head.

Gordon and Shane dragged Randy's body to the base of a huge sand pile. Shane then went to the trunk of their vehicle and retrieved a short-handled shovel and a fifty-pound bag of lime that Gordon had picked up at a local hardware store earlier in the week, in anticipation of Randy's killing. Both Gordon and Shane took turns clearing a spot large enough to secret Randy's body, at the base of a huge pile of sand. Together, they rolled Randy's lifeless body into the void they had created with the shovel. Randy's body dropped into the cleared space precisely, face-up.

Gordon ripped the bag of lime open and poured it all over Randy's body, first covering his head and upper torso, and then the rest of his body. As Gordon was pouring the lime onto Randy's body, he told Shane that he had read in a book that lime would speed up human decomposition and reduce the odor of the decomposing body. When the bag was empty, they covered Randy's body with sand. Gordon carried the empty lime bag back to the car, and threw it in the trunk.

Within two weeks of Randy's murder, Gordon and Shane set Gordon's property on fire. The commercial building burned to the ground, but St. Andrew's firefighters had been suspicious about the cause of the fire after they found a burned-up, plastic gasoline container inside the remainder of a burned-out storage area near the back of the building, so they contacted a State Fire Marshal.

As with all suspected arson investigations, the Fire Marshal's office placed signs near the site of the fire, offering a five-thousand-dollar reward for information leading to the successful resolution and apprehension of suspect(s) responsible for the fire.

According to police reports, Gordon and Shane returned to the sandpit twice a week, following Randy's murder, uncovered his body, and sprinkled more lime on it, before covering up his remains with sand again. Gordon and Shane were finally arrested at the sandpit, performing their biweekly ritual, after police set up surveillance on the site.

It turned out that Shane, like Randy, also couldn't keep his mouth shut. He had bragged to a fellow bar patron at one of the local taverns, about the arson, and how he and Gordon had murdered Randy and disposed of his body. Shane told the guy that Randy had been one of the original players in the insurance fraud scheme, but that he had proven untrustworthy, and had to be eliminated. Shane even told him about putting the lime on Randy's body and how they continued doing that twice a week.

The bar patron he had bragged to had seen the posters offering a five-thousand-dollar reward around town. In his mind, five thousand dollars was a lot of money. In a subsequent interview, he described receiving the reward money as similar to "winning the lottery". He was happy to cash in on Shane's disclosure, and he promptly went straight to the police for a trade of his information for the reward. It all worked out for him, but for Gordon and Shane, not so much.

Following Shane and Gordon's murder and arson trial, Gordon was sentenced to 19 years to life in prison, and Shane received a sentence of 12 to 50 years for his role in the arson and the murder of Randy Pitco.

12

ON MAY 16, 1981, FOLLOWING THE JOHNSON STREET PARK ATTACK, the Waterford Police Department had a tip line installed at the police station, specifically so that callers, who believed that they may have information about the crime and the possible suspects, could report their information.

Hundreds of telephone calls poured in, in the short time that the phone line had been established. The police Dispatcher would answer the call and then forward the tip to Deputy Prosecutor Corey Degree for review and evaluation. If there was any possibility that the caller's information had some value or validity, it was his job to get it to Sgt. Spano, so that he could assign someone to follow up on the information.

By the time Detective Smart and I had finished interviewing Randy Pitco and released him, we learned that two investigators, Detective Josh Able and Cpl. Allan Coons, had been assigned to follow up on a telephone call received from Tony Hampton's grandmother, Margaret Hampton. She lived in Banbury with her son, Gerald, and his family, which included Tony Hampton. Immediately after receiving the telephone call, Sgt. Spano assigned Detective Josh Able and Cpl. Allan Coons to go to Mrs. Hampton's home in Banbury and interview her.

Able and Coons would later tell us that Mrs. Hampton explained to the investigators that she was a "born again Christian," and that she tried to live and practice her faith every day, in every way. Mrs. Hampton said that her faith required her to 'hate the sin and love the sinner'.

She told the investigators that after seeing the suspects' sketches on the news and considering Tony's inexplicable behavior on the late afternoon of the very same day of the Johnson Street Park attack, and the fact that Tony had been acting very differently since that day, which was out of character for him, she suspected he may have been involved in that attack.

She told the investigators that she had prayed about what she should do with her information about her grandson. She said that even though Tony was her grandson, she could not, in good conscience keep this information to herself. She said she felt compelled to relay this information to the officers investigating this horrible crime.

With that, she started crying and then said, "I think you should look at Tony for this crime." She continued to cry and kept saying, "May God have mercy on his soul."

After regaining her composure, Mrs. Hampton provided some background information on her grandson, revealing his age, the school he attended in Banbury, and information about Tony's odd personality quirks. She told Detective Able and Cpl. Coons that Tony was sixteen years old and went to Banbury High School. He was pleasant enough most of the time, but could be moody, and sometimes he said stupid things and talked as if he were crazy. She had seen Tony be mean to the family dog on a number of occasions, punching and choking the poor thing. Mrs. Hampton told the two of them that she had stepped in on a number of those occasions, trying to protect the dog, and Tony had sworn at her and pushed her around. On one occasion, she said that she thought Tony was going to hit her.

Mrs. Hampton said that she had told Tony's father, Gerald, and that he was supposed to address her concerns with Tony, but she did not believe that he ever did, because if he had, Tony would have probably been mean to her, or made threats to her for telling his father.

She said that there were other times when Tony would be kind and affectionate towards the dog. Mrs. Hampton added that Tony had a pellet rifle that he used to shoot small animals with. She said that she had seen him shoot squirrels, chipmunks, pigeons, and on at least two occasions, neighborhood cats and dogs. On many of those occasions, the animal did not die instantly upon being shot, so Tony would go into the yard with a wooden baseball bat and finish the wounded animal or bird off. She said that on those occasions, he acted crazy while he was bludgeoning the helpless thing to death… Hitting it again and again with the bat.

Gerald had taken Tony with him to a cousin's home in Langford County, to help slaughter some pigs on the Saturday before the Johnson Street Park attack, and that Mrs. Hampton felt that Tony was amused by the killing and butchering of the hogs because that seemed to be all that he talked about since.

She then told the investigators that Tony came home on May 15, the day of the Johnson Street Park, attack, and changed his clothes immediately. Tony had put the clothes he had just taken off in the washing machine and washed them right away, which was suspicious in and of itself, because it was so unusual. He had never done any laundry—not even for himself, and not in his entire life. In the past, when Tony had wanted or needed something washed, he had always asked his mother or her to wash them.

Mrs. Hampton said that even though Tony was only sixteen years old, he had a heavy beard for such a young man. Tony had kept a full beard until that incident in Waterford. But that day, right after he threw his clothes in the washing machine, he had gone into the bathroom and shaved off his beard. She went on to describe a comment that Tony had made after seeing a local news broadcast about the Johnson Street Park attack. Tony had commented about how awful that crime was, and how he wondered if the people who did it would ever be caught. This was odd, because Tony never watched the news, and she had never heard him comment or show any interest in anything related to news, or local events before this. She said that all by itself, his comment was probably harmless, but that she just found his interest in that story and his comment very peculiar.

During the conversation with the two investigators, Mrs. Hampton had also described Tony's newest sidekick as a kid named John Pitco, who was younger than Tony. She said he was skinny, with blonde hair and a pimply face. She added that he lived in Waterford, not far from the park where the attack had occurred. She said she knew that from overhearing John and Tony talking. She told Able and Coons that John was another reason for her suspicion about Tony being involved—John definitely looked like the boy in the sketch of the blonde-haired suspect—and he lived close to the park where this had happened.

She closed their interview by telling Able and Coons that she felt like a tremendous burden had been lifted off her because she had shared her information with them. She said that she had "been praying for those two girls and their families," ever since she had learned about the attack.

After interviewing Mrs. Hampton, and before leaving Banbury, investigators Able and Coons dropped by the Banbury High School, and managed to obtain a recent school yearbook with Tony's picture in it. The photo in the yearbook was of Tony with his beard, and he looked just like the sketch of the dark-haired suspect. That picture of Tony, in the yearbook, was photographed by police technicians, and would later be used in a suspect photo lineup.

13

WENDY WAS STILL AT THE HOSPITAL IN INTENSIVE CARE WHEN detectives presented her with two separate photo lineups. One of the lineups had photos of eight dark-haired males with beards, including Tony Hampton's reproduced photograph from the Banbury High School yearbook.

The second photo lineup was of eight blonde-haired males, which included the school photograph of John Pitco given to us by his brother, Randy.

Wendy was told to take her time and not try to identify anyone if she was not sure of herself. Detectives said that her hands were trembling when they were handed to her. They were each handed to her separately. Wendy did take her time. She stared intently at each of the two photo lineups. She slowly and methodically reviewed each of the photographs in both of the lineups prepared by the detectives and given to her to view.

Everyone in the room held their breath and watched intensely. Wendy's hands began to tremble even more and her eyes filled with tears as she pointed out Tony Hampton's photo from the other dark-haired males. She said, "That's the dark-haired man. I'm certain. He killed Stacie." She then pointed to John Pitco's photo from the second lineup. Still trembling and crying, she said, "He is the blonde-haired man that raped me." She grabbed her face with both hands and covered her eyes as she wept with everything that was in her. Wendy wept so loudly that hospital staff and physicians on her floor rushed to the doorway of her room. The officers said that everyone—police, medical staff, and physicians alike—had tears streaming down their faces.

Even though everyone in the room was teary-eyed, they were all silently cheering on the inside. With this development, we had the suspects now. One of the detectives at the hospital called the station on the phone and told Sgt. Spano what had just happened. He in turn relayed that information to all of us.

Everyone cheered out loud. We had the bastards. Sure, there was plenty of work left to do, but we would see to it that nothing got screwed up. Wendy had come through, like the champion we had all come to know her to be. All of our collective efforts thus far were not in vain. We now just had to make sure that no one messed this case up, moving forward.

The detectives rushed back to the police station and went to work typing affidavits, search warrant applications, police reports, non-testimonial order requests, etc. Everyone connected with this case worked all afternoon and into the early evening, chasing details, doing follow-up, and preparing all of the required paperwork. While this was underway, others started collecting and organizing the equipment, forms, and evidence collection items that would be required to carry out the impending raids and arrest. We wanted to make sure that we dotted all our i's and crossed all of our t's. We had no intention of losing any of this on some technicality. It was one of the few times none of us bitched about all of the tedious paperwork that is required on a major case like this. We wanted this case to be airtight.

After several hours had passed and all of the paperwork was completed and reviewed, State's Attorney Banfield, Detective Sgts. Spano and Green got on the telephone. They made separate telephone calls until they found a judge who agreed to review their paperwork and potentially sign the non-testimonial orders and search and arrest warrants.

As soon as they found one, off they went, with their completed paperwork in hand. Two hours later they returned, with signed search and arrest warrants and non-testimonial evidence orders for John Pitco and John's parents' residence in Waterford, and Tony Hampton and Tony's parents' residence in Banbury.

Officers were selected and assigned to each of the two separate Search and Arrest teams and operations plans were developed by each team, for the impending raids. The officer and detective assignments to the two teams answered the questions about who would be on which team and what each officer's role would be on their team. The plans were detailed and required precise and simultaneous execution of the two search warrants, both at the same time to avoid anyone from being tipped off or alerted. We were all ready and no one wanted to be left out of these final operations to wrap up the case, arrest the bad guys, and bring justice to the victims.

14

I HAD WAITED PATIENTLY TO LEARN WHAT MY ROLE WOULD BE AND which team I would be on, but just before the announcement, I was taken aside by Detective Sgt. Green and told that I would not be on either of the teams. I was directed to wait at the Vermont State Police barracks, where the two suspects would be transported following their arrest. Sgt. Green said that he wanted me there when the younger suspect was brought in. It would be my job to guard John Pitco, specifically from the other officers, whose emotions and anger levels towards the suspects had increased throughout the investigation and had grown substantially through the day.

My instructions were not to allow anyone to say anything to the offenders. He pointed out that it went without saying that no one was to touch John or Tony in any way either. I acknowledged his orders and set out to ready myself for my impending assignment.

I must admit that when I was first told by Sgt. Green about my assignment, I was disappointed that I wouldn't be part of one of the two raid teams, but I quickly realized that everyone had a role to play, and my role would be every bit as important as the events now leading to the arrest of both suspects and the searches of their respective homes. This would not be the most glamorous assignment that I would ever be given or be responsible for, but it was important and necessary. I knew this would be a tough assignment, but understood the importance of not letting anything compromise our case.

There were suspect detention officers assigned to each team, whose job would be to secure and watch over each of the suspects in their respective homes until the search of each of the premises was completed. There were team search officers with evidence collection assignments, as well as a team photographer, a team videographer, and four site security officers on each team.

When the searches were done, both suspects would be escorted back to the Neary County State Police barracks, where the evidence outlined in the non-testimonial evidence orders would be collected, and recorded interviews would be conducted with each of them.

By the time the teams were established and each team had developed their team assignments, and conducted a walk-through rehearsal of each team's plans, it was after 10 pm. The two teams were now moving to predetermined locations close to their target's homes and at precisely 10:45 pm, both teams would simultaneously execute their search warrants.

I watched as the two Search and Arrest team convoys loaded their vehicles and drove out-of-sight from the police station driveway. I then found my way to my assigned vehicle, and drove to the Neary County State Police barracks across town, where they planned to return with the suspects following the searches and each suspect's arrest.

I couldn't help but think about the past seventy-two hours. The emergency phone call to the police station, the Dispatcher's face, the little girl who I initially thought was wearing a red dress because she was covered in her own blood from her neck to her knees, and the railroad conductor... That exhausting run down the railroad tracks, walking that footpath from the railroad tracks into the back of the park, and Officer Killen's calling out to me, "Over here. I found her." I vividly recalled pushing my way through the brush on the second footpath and discovering the clearing at the crime scene... And, seeing Stacie's tortured body under that dirty, blood-stained mattress and checking her lifeless body for a pulse.

I relived every moment and thought about the events that had transpired since the day of the attack. How I had searched the traffic ticket and moving violation files and found the defective equipment ticket for the blue station wagon. matching that vehicle to the suspicious vehicle, and vehicle occupants described by Tracey Wells in the adjacent community of Middleton Falls during the evening following the attack.

I recalled tracking down and finding Randy Pitco, and the interview with him that followed, and getting him to obtain the photo of John Pitco from his residence. I recalled all of the shared information that Tony's grandmother had provided. Then the photo line-up, and the onslaught of police activity at the station this afternoon and evening.

Throughout all of this, my mind kept flashing back to the victims, their small bodies and the horrible things that they had endured. In my mind's eye, I could still see Stacie's face when I had rolled her up on her side and checked her for any signs of life there in that clearing, under that disgustingly filthy mattress. I replayed in my head the unthinkable things that Tony and John did to those poor girls. In my mind, I kept comparing the two small victims to my eight-year-old daughter, Annie. I was angry at my mind's insistence on comparing those two small girls to Annie, but no matter how hard I tried, I could not stop myself from doing it.

When I arrived at the Vermont State Police barracks I went inside and prepared for the impending arrival of the suspects. After nearly three hours, I heard the Search and Arrest teams call on the radio and report that they were on their way to the Neary County State Police barracks with the two suspects.

It turned out that—just as I thought—this was one of the toughest assignments I had ever been given. For I too had strong feelings of anger and disgust for these two men but I had to control myself, and keep my thoughts to myself.

The sight of John, with that fixed smirk on his face, infuriated me, but I reminded myself not to let this case get away from us. The satisfaction of a two-second or even a two-minute outburst would be short-lived, and the consequences would potentially last a lifetime and would be unthinkable for everyone, especially Stacie and Wendy's families.

15

When the two teams arrived back at the State Police Barracks, we all learned that at Tony's residence, the team executing the search warrant had found a locked door to a small room in the basement of the Hampton residence belonging to Tony's father, Gerald Hampton.

Once the search team managed to get inside, they found dozens of photographs of naked children engaged in a variety of sexual acts. The search team found child pornography strewn throughout the room. Many of the photos were of Gerald's nine-year-old daughter and her eight-year-old girlfriend and playmate. The photos included a nude Gerald Hampton with his naked daughter and her young girlfriend in various poses, staged in sexually suggestive sex acts.

Tony's father, Gerald Hampton, was arrested at the scene and lodged at the Neary County Correctional Center. His nine-year-old daughter and the other underage children living in the Hampton home were immediately taken into protective custody and released to the Vermont Department of Child Welfare, and placed in temporary housing and foster homes.

Tony's grandmother and the mother of Gerald Hampton insisted that she had no inkling of the room or her son's prurient photographic interest.

Gerald would later be tried and convicted in May 1982 of several felony sex crimes involving possession of child pornography and manufacturing child pornography, involving his daughter and his daughter's playmate. He was sentenced to six to fifteen years in prison for those crimes.

When the search team entered Tony's bedroom, on the top of the night-stand next to his bed, they found a *True Detective* magazine with a cover headline story titled 'The rape, torture, and murder of a twelve-year-old girl' lying in plain view, as if it had been read, or was still being read.

While this magazine story was not a story about the May 15, 1981 attack in Waterford, Vermont, but more likely than not, it was the story that inspired or motivated Tony and John to attack, torture and rape the two girls in the woods at the Johnson Street Park.

Magazines like this were plentiful and prevalent at newsstands every-where in the late seventies and early eighties. They generally were filled with sensationalized headlines and contained bizarre and shocking tales about crimes and unimaginable cruelty. These types of magazines were found among the many tabloid newspapers that carried equally bizarre and dis-turbing stories.

The Hampton residence search team had also found the laundered clothes that Tony Hampton had worn during the attack in the park, in Tony's bedroom—the clothes that his grandmother had described seeing him change out of and wash on the day the girls were attacked.

The Pitco residence search team discovered and seized four boxes of pellet gun ammunition from John's bedroom, but no actual pellet pistols. They had also located and recovered John's laundered clothes, worn by him during the attack at the park. All of the located and seized items at the Pitco home were found in John's bedroom, except for a steak knife which was recovered in the kitchen of the Pitco residence. The search team had located four wooden-handled, serrated-edged, steak knives, identical to the one found in the Johnson Street Park by Cpl. Lance Buckman.

Both young suspects—John Pitco, age fifteen, and Tony Hampton, age sixteen—were taken into custody at their respective homes and transported to the Neary County State Police barracks, where a team of additional inves-tigators and evidence collection technicians awaited their arrival.

Having heard the news about what the search teams had located and seized at the Hampton and Pitco residences, I found myself feeling pretty good about the growing strength of our case against the duo.

Just like everyone else, I was appalled by the description of the magazine found on the nightstand in Tony's bedroom, and I was fairly surprised by the news of Tony's father's secret room in the basement and his victimization of his nine-year-old daughter and her girlfriend. But I was pleased that it was discovered, and that Tony's father was arrested on the spot for it.

Every police officer and social services worker knows and accepts that when abusive conduct or behavior is witnessed over and over again, it can often be mentally imprinted or become learned behavior to those subjected to it, or witnessing it. That behavior, in turn, can then be carried from one generation to another. Many documented cases have shown us this fact. However, none of us had ever imagined that sexual depravity might also be so prevalent in the Hampton family home that it quite possibly became learned behavior for Tony Hampton. At the very least, it probably influenced Tony's prurient curiosity and interest.

We all worked straight through the night. By morning we had the two suspects under arrest with full confessions and the collected non-testimonial evidence that had been ordered taken by the courts.

I was relieved that I never had any problems with any of the other officers or detectives throughout the night. Some of them did come around to get a look at John in person, but when I took them aside and told them that I was assigned to protect him and ward off any inappropriate remarks, they had each said that they understood and no one presented any problems. They were all disgusted but relieved that we had identified, tracked down, and arrested the individuals responsible for this horrendous crime. They had all said that they certainly did not want to be responsible for giving John or Tony any reason to claim that their rights had been violated. I think it's safe to say that every one of us was shocked by the young age of the girls' attackers and the brutality that they had each demonstrated in executing their crimes.

At daybreak, Detective Sgt. Spano called me aside to tell me that Sgt. Bedard and I were going to be tasked with bringing John back over to the Johnson Street Park, where he would show us where he and Tony had buried the missing evidence from the May 15th attack.

In his confession, John had said that he and Tony ran a short distance from where they committed the crime to an area, still in the woods at Johnson Street Park, but away from the actual crime scene, dug a hole with their hands and buried most of the items immediately after the attack of the two girls. The duo then fled from the park.

When we walked John out of the Neary County State Police barracks, there were reporters everywhere with TV cameras on, the flashing cameras lighting up the early morning parking lot. Reporters were calling out to John, trying to get him to say something, but he did not speak to them. He held his head down and wouldn't even look in their direction.

I held onto John's left arm and Sgt. Bedard held onto his right arm, as we walked him to our waiting cruiser. At one point, I had to use my right arm to block a reporter from pushing me to try to get closer to John. I could see that John was visibly shaken. His heart was pounding so hard that I could see it beating through his shirt. I could also see his chest heaving as his breathing sped up and his pulse rate increased. By the time Sgt. Bedard and I got John into the backseat of the cruiser and shut the car door, John was shaken. Both of us noticed that his hands were trembling and his palms were sweaty.

Once in the safety of the rear seat of the cruiser, John breathed a sigh of relief and said that the reporters had scared him. I almost choked on what he had said and I quickly retorted that maybe that's how scared the girls in the park were. He glared at me with a fixed smirk on his face. I immediately caught myself and realized that I couldn't allow myself to be manipulated by this lowlife. I forced myself to calm down and refrain from reacting to anything John said. I could not allow myself to say the things that I felt like saying to him. I remained quiet and did not speak further to John during the rest of the ride to the park.

Once at the Johnson Street Park, both Sgt. Bedard and I removed John from the backseat and held onto his handcuffed arms as he directed us to the secret burial site in the back of the park, a short distance from the railroad tracks. John led us to a steep bank, west of the clearing, where he and Tony had attacked the girls. This location was a short distance north of the railroad tracks, and approximately one hundred yards west of where the attack had taken place. John pointed to a large dirt patch near the top of the bank that appeared to have been freshly disturbed. The grass and ground cover were missing, and there was loose dirt lying on top of the spot that John had identified. The dirt spot formed a circle about three or four feet in diameter.

Other officers were standing by with shovels and rakes, and once the spot was photographed, they carefully excavated it. Sgt. Bedard and I stood by with John still tightly in our grasp, while they carefully dug in the spot identified by him. Approximately two feet below the surface, they found what we had come here looking for. The girls' missing articles of clothing—both of the girls' jeans, their blouses, shoes, and their underwear, along with two unmatching knee socks.

As they now dug in the dirt with their bare hands, they also found the second wooden-handled, bloodstained kitchen knife, that matched the earlier one found by Cpl. Lance Buckman mixed in with the girls' buried personal items, along with the two missing pellet guns that looked like .357 Magnum revolvers. Everything was buried here together. Now we knew why John had stolen Randy's pellet gun. So that he and Tony would each have one for this crime.

Evidence technicians were brought in, and they systematically collected and tagged all of the dug-up evidence and processed the burial site for any trace evidence that might have been left behind by the suspects.

Sgt. Bedard and I walked John back to the parked cruiser, secured him in the backseat, and drove back to the police station. On the ride to the station, John acted very pleased with himself for showing us where he and Tony had hidden the girls' things and murder weapons. He wore that stupid smirk on his face like he always did, as if to say, 'see, I told you I could take you to the buried things you were looking for'. As angry as his demeanor and attitude made me, I chalked his goofy conduct up to his Autism Spectrum Disorder. Nevertheless, I was too angry to feel sorry for him.

When we arrived at the police station, there was a small crowd of reporters waiting outside the backdoor. Sgt. Bedard and I removed John from the rear of the cruiser and escorted him into the police station through the backdoor. Cameras were clicking and reporters once again shouted questions to John, just as they had this morning at the State Police barracks. As earlier, John kept his head down and did not respond to anything that they said.

Inside the station, everything was being finalized and arraignment paperwork was being organized and prepared. I saw at least two officers catching a little shut-eye in squad room chairs. There was fresh coffee, bagels, doughnuts, and breakfast sandwiches spread out on a table in the detective's office, and we were encouraged to take a break and grab something to eat, after we locked up John in one of the two holding cells.

Chief Whitmore came walking down the hallway, shaking all the officers' hands and thanking them for all that they had contributed to the investigation. When he got to me in the hallway, he shook my hand, and said, "We chose the right person to be our next detective. This was a tough one, even for the most seasoned officers on the case. I heard about everything you did, your willingness to do the things you were tasked with, even when those tasks were not flashy and exciting, and I heard about all the hours you voluntarily worked. Never bitching or complaining. I appreciate everything you did, and when it's time for future promotions, I will remember all of this as well." He ended by saying, "I'm proud to have you on my team. Good job." I humbly thanked him and stepped out of his way, so that he could continue down the hallway, shaking hands and thanking all the members of our investigation team.

By midday, all of the required arraignment paperwork was complete and some precautionary telephone calls were made to the courthouse and State's Attorney's Office so that they could ensure that appropriate safety precautions and security measures were in place before the arrival of Tony and John.

At 1 pm, Tony and John were escorted from the police station to awaiting police cruisers in handcuffs. They were walked individually and slowly to ensure that the holed-up media, camped out behind the police station, could spring into action, snapping pictures of the duo while the television station reporters shot live video footage of them. There was a chorus of reporters shouting questions to both of the suspects as they were walked to the cruisers. "Where are you taking them?" one voiced called out. "To the Neary County Court House, where they will be arraigned," announced one of the officers escorting Tony. The two men kept their heads down so that none of the reporters could get a direct photograph of either of their faces, and neither of them responded to any of the reporters' questions.

The two men were then transported to the Neary County Courthouse, in Banbury, for immediate court arraignments. Troopers from the Vermont State Police and Sheriff's Deputies, from the Neary County Sheriff's Department, dispatched additional police officers to the building. State's Attorney Banfield was very concerned that the arriving suspects may be greeted by angry family members, friends, and outraged Vermonters. The detailed officers formed a human corridor from the transport cruisers to the courtroom, where the two men were each arraigned on murder, attempted murder, aggravated assault, aggravated sexual assault, abduction, and a variety of other, lesser included offenses.

The Banbury Free Press would report the next day that a crowd estimated to be more than seventy-five people had assembled outside the Neary County Court House, just so they could get a look at Tony and John. Other than cursing and calling them each some derogatory names, no one tried to physically do anything to either of the suspects.

Ultimately, however, John Pitco would be charged as a juvenile delinquent because he was only 15 years old, while Tony Hampton would be charged as an adult because he was 16 years old. It was a technicality in Vermont law that would be changed before summer's end.

The judge ordered both of them held without bail and remanded them each into state custody.

Individual officers and detectives who had dealt directly with Wendy and Stacie's families, drove to the Whitcomb residence to tell them about the arrest and arraignments. Wendy Redding was still in the hospital, so officers went there as well to inform her family about the developments. Officers at the hospital said that Wendy cried and trembled uncontrollably as she expressed her relief that the suspects had been caught. They said she could be heard through the hospital corridor. The physicians and nursing staff gathered at her open hospital room door to show their empathy and support. There were no dry eyes in Wendy's room, and in the hospital corridor, for that matter.

Wendy and her family cried together for a long time. It may have been the first time that Wendy cried for herself and her best friend Stacie. All of us believed that Wendy had been so determined to get the men who did this to her and her friend that she may not have taken any time to grieve earlier.

Within a few hours of the news of John and Tony's arrest being circulated in the media, people were driving by the police station blowing their horns and shouting their approval and praise for the work that the police had done. Handmade signs and banners were erected along the street in front of the Waterford Police Station and over at the Johnson Street Park proclaiming that our citizens and community were proud of its police department. Commercial billboards along the roadways throughout the region were flashing messages of praise and pride in their police. People, including Governor Richard Snelling and many Vermont State Legislatures, were offering high praise to all of the officers who had worked so tirelessly on this case. Platters of food and fresh baked goods began arriving at the Waterford Police Station as soon as the news became public, and the food continued arriving for a week. When the public learned that every police department in Neary County had participated in the investigation in one way or another, food and baked goods from appreciative residents were brought into every police station in the County.

Over the next several hours, the police station telephone lines lit up with reporters and media outlets from across the nation offering praise and making inquiries about the crime and arrests. Vermont's two Congressional Senators and our only Congressman also called to thank all of the officers as well.

16

ONCE I WAS SURE THAT JOHN AND TONY HAD BEEN ARRAIGNED and remanded into state custody, I breathed a sigh of relief. In my mind, I kept thinking of the time when I saw little Wendy Redding, and believed that she was wearing a red dress… and the shock of discovering that she was not wearing anything, and that her own blood had created the illusion of the dress. That image has haunted me through the years. When I close my eyes and think back, I still see the little girl in a red dress, being helped along by Mr. Thompson.

It's interesting and a little peculiar how a person's mind can sometimes play tricks on them. Over the years, I have worked on a huge variety of criminal cases. There have been a handful of times, when I first arrived on a crime scene or saw something or someone in a criminal setting for the first time, and I had a thought pop into my head about what the image I was seeing was, or what it represented. Later on, when I was able to see the same image or person more clearly and in the appropriate context, my initial thought(s) were proven incorrect.

In every case, however, there was a logical explanation for why my mind initially arrived at the incorrect conclusion that it had.

I left the office and headed home to see my family. I was exhausted, mentally and physically. I was fairly certain that all of the other officers felt the same way. It had been an exhaustive week. On my ride home, I decided to make a slight diversion from my usual route and drove to a small clearing in the woods, just off the main road, in my hometown of Waynesville. It was a place that I had visited many times growing up. Sometimes to be alone with a girl, or sometimes, just to be alone. It was peaceful and quiet there. There was no one around, and there were no homes nearby, so I felt comfortable that there wasn't anyone in the vicinity.

I parked the car and shut off the engine, and just stared up at the sky. Once again, my mind began racing with all that had happened over the past few days. Thoughts and images of the girls and their horrific injuries, the crime scene, and the faces of the suspects flooded my mind, and I could not hold it back any longer.

Every time I thought about Wendy Redding, I could see her in the red dress that I had initially perceived her to be wearing when we first met. I wept. I wept for the victims, for their parents, and for the families of the victims. I wept because of the shock and horror of this senseless crime, and I wept for me. I knew that I would never be the same again and that I would never be able to shake these internal thoughts and memories. I would carry these memories and images in my mind for eternity.

I wept for what seemed like a very long time, and when I was done, I took my first deep breath since this bizarre incident unfolded on May 15th. It felt as though my chest had just fully inflated for the first time since it had all started. Even though it had only been four days, it felt like forever since I had drawn a breath that deep. That's when I noticed that I had wept so hard that my whole body was trembling and my hands were shaking uncontrollably.

I would never let anyone see me like this, and I have never told anyone about this—until now. I had held back those tears on many occasions since this tragic attack and I just needed to release them. Open the flood gates and get it out of my system. Then I could go back to my stoic police officer persona.

After waiting there, for another fifteen minutes, my eyes dried and I stopped trembling. I checked in the rearview mirror to make sure that the swelling and redness in my face and eyes had gone away and I looked okay, so that I could continue my drive the rest of the way home.

Grown men in my family did not cry. Neither did police officers, at that time. We learned early on that we had to be emotionally strong and never talked about, or revealed our true feelings at or on the job.

Thankfully, things have changed as our profession and culture have become more enlightened. I wouldn't learn for years that most of the officers and detectives who had worked on this case, had similar experiences, away from everyone else and out of everyone else's sight.

Nowadays, we teach young police officers that it is perfectly normal to feel bad or sad when confronted with tragedies and unspeakable crimes and victim images. In modern police departments, officers are taught that once the emergent circumstances of a case or incident have passed, and they find themselves in the safety of the police station or their cruiser, they should acknowledge their emotions and deal with their feelings through a host of prescribed programs and revolutionary new police support practices, including professional counselors, who specifically treat and council emergency responders.

However, in 1981, the law enforcement community and its culture were not nearly as enlightened and tolerant of such things. In those days, police officers that showed any signs of weakness and emotion were not looked upon favorably by the other officers in the department. Those personal traits were seen as signs of weakness. Even officers who became sick to their stomach at a police incident or crime scene, lest there was an exceptional reason, were either laughed at and picked on, or they were given unflattering nicknames by the other officers that would follow them through his or her, career. In some cases, they found that their career path became much narrower, with fewer opportunities for new assignments or advancement.

When I arrived home, my wife and kids met me in the driveway. We hugged and high-fived. I felt horrible for the Redding and Whitcomb families, but thankful for my own family and thankful that my family was safe. I stayed outside and played with Jared and Annie for a while, as I thought about how I would feel if something happened to one or both of them. I had deep feelings of guilt for thinking like that and feeling that way.

Many neighbors, friends, and family members stopped by to show their support and thanked me and asked me to pass along their gratitude and appreciation to all of the other officers, for everything that we had done. After hearing this time and again, Annie asked me about what had happened and if that is why I had been sad lately. I told her that I had been sad, and that someday, when she was older, I would tell her all about it. She seemed satisfied with that answer. I never did do that. I guess she will have to read it here—in this book. My sincere apologies to Annie.

I didn't sleep at all that night. But, then again, I didn't sleep for many nights following that incident. Sometimes when I did fall asleep, I would suddenly be startled awake as I relived those horrible events and the crime and the investigation that followed. I would regularly fall asleep briefly, only to be awakened or startled by a bad dream about that day and that horrible crime. Sometimes, in my dreams, when I lifted that dirty mattress in the clearing, I found my daughter Annie lying there, instead of Stacie.

I would instantly wake up, shaken by the nightmare. I would then make myself stay awake for the rest of the night, so my mind wouldn't return to that nightmare again. In several of those bad dreams, when I saw Wendy covered in blood, it would be my daughter, Annie instead of Wendy. It took years and years for those nightmares to stop.

Thinking back, it felt like every time I closed my eyes, I could see Wendy and Stacie's faces in my mind over and over again. Especially Stacie. I have silently mourned for her every day of my life since May 15, 1981. Even when I think about her today, I still get all choked up.

Since that day, I have never been able to pass by the intersection of Elm and Johnson Street, or the Johnson Street Park, without my mind flashing back to that day, and remembering the two girls. I doubt that I ever will be able to.

Sometimes it's the faces of John and Tony that haunt my innermost thoughts. Each time it happens to me, it brings me right back to that day in the Johnson Street Park and that crime scene. If I let myself, I can still feel the raindrops landing on my face and head, as I relive standing in that small opening, next to Stacie's lifeless body.

Eventually, I would learn to compartmentalize this incident, which I have tucked into the dark recesses of my mind. It felt like the only way I could move on. I did not know it at that time, but I would go on to see and store hundreds of cases, faces, and unpleasant memories in that same compartment, deep in my mind, before finishing my forty-six-year career in law enforcement. I think that if my mind was a computer, I would have run out of storage space in that secret compartment a long time ago.

A year after the attack, my wife Carol bought Annie a pretty, red, velvet dress to wear on Christmas day. I remember the first time that I saw Annie wearing that red dress and the anxiety that it produced within me. Though Annie looked like an angel when she was wearing it, my mind flashed back to the horrible sight of Wendy Redding in "a red dress," the first time that I ever saw her. I never said anything, but I was happy when Annie outgrew the dress. Even now, whenever I see a young girl wearing a red dress, I can't help but think back to that day, and the images of the two girls.

I have always been saddened by the memories associated with this case, but proud to have been part of the team that promptly and efficiently went from having no suspects to identifying and arresting those responsible, in only four short days. When we were confronted with this horrible crime and the almost overwhelming challenges of solving the case and finding the individuals responsible for this unthinkable attack, we all rose to the occasion and through all of our collective efforts, we managed to bring John and Tony to justice, and we accomplished that in only four days. I learned a lesson through all of this that I would never forget and apply many times during my law enforcement career. When we all put our petty differences aside and check our ego at the door, we can do great things, working together as a team.

Years later, when I became the Criminal Division Commander and we would have other major criminal investigations, I pointed to that lesson whenever I conducted the initial investigative team meeting and briefing, I shared that lesson with the entire team, and it worked each time.

17

IN THE DAYS AND WEEKS FOLLOWING THE ATTACK AND ARRESTS OF John and Tony, Vermont citizens began expressing their outrage and anger that John Pitco would only be charged as a juvenile delinquent due to his age. Even after his conviction, John would be held in a juvenile rehabilitation center for only three years. On John's eighteenth birthday, he would have to be released.

People were angry that John and Tony would not be held equally responsible for the attacks and the death of Stacie Whitcomb, and both would not receive the same punishment.

Under Vermont law at that time, fifteen-year-old defendants were treated as juvenile delinquents, regardless of their crime. They also could not be incarcerated or held for any delinquent acts they had been convicted of, once they reached the legal age of majority. When John Pitco turned eighteen years old, under Vermont law, he would be released from juvenile rehabilitation.

A public outcry and a citizen uprising of sorts began. Vermont citizens were demanding that the Governor recall the State's part-time legislature to address the disparities in the existing law that would send one man to prison for life and the other into a residential juvenile facility for three years when they were both guilty of committing the same crimes. Vermonters wanted both men locked up for the rest of their lives, for what they had done.

Governor Richard Snelling said that it couldn't be done. But the citizens learned that there was a provision under Vermont law that allowed the

Governor to call for a special session through a proclamation that sets out the necessity for convening such a session, to reconsider and amend the law that would set John Pitco free when he turned eighteen years old. It never crossed anyone's mind that even if the Governor recalled the Legislature and the law was changed, that it would not apply to John Pitco because his crime was committed before any new law or revision that would be enacted.

Governor Snelling refused to recall the Legislature. Many Vermonters were angered by this, and they began demanding that the Governor recall the state's Legislature to consider new laws that would allow juvenile killers to be charged as adults. Small protests near his office and home were staged with increasing regularity. Despite the growing number of Vermonters who wanted this to happen, Governor Snelling held fast and defiantly refused to recall the Legislature and Senate for a special, summer session.

That would all change when two Waterford mothers, whose daughters had been friends with Wendy Redding and Stacie Whitcomb, refused to accept the Governor's decision and started a petition drive in Waterford Village to force the Governor to recall the Legislature to address this issue. Citizens across Vermont were equally incensed by the Governor's arrogance and refusal to recall the Legislature, so communities across Vermont replicated the Waterford petition drive. Every day the petition drive received so much attention in the news that Vermonters in towns and cities, small and large, across the entire state adopted similar petitions, collecting thousands of signatures of registered Vermont voters who demanded that the Governor recall the Legislature. After a prolonged battle between the Governor and Vermont's citizens, the Governor finally recalled the Legislature, but only after he felt he had been forced to do so, and on the advice of his closest political advisors.

As a result of the recall, Legislatures crafted a new juvenile law that was promptly signed into law and enacted. In this amended statute, a juvenile offender could be charged as an adult when they committed certain serious crimes—murder being the first and foremost. With the revised law, a juvenile offender, at least eleven-years-old, could be sentenced to incarceration, just like an adult offender, with no regard for, or consideration of their age. If convicted under this revised law, the juvenile offender would be held in a juvenile detention facility until their eighteenth birthday, and then transferred to an adult facility, for the length of their sentence.

Not only was the law changed in Vermont, but when the citizens learned from Governor Snelling's mouth that the law didn't make much difference, because Vermont had no juvenile detention facility large enough to hold more than two or three delinquent youths at one time, the citizens demanded that the State build a new juvenile detention center to hold such serious criminal offenders.

After months of Legislative squabbling and an exhaustive number of public debates, a new juvenile detention facility, appropriately sized, was finally approved. It was built in the mid-1980s, in the Town of Waterford, across from a former military base, in a rural part of the community. The facility was named the Woodside Juvenile Detention and Rehabilitation Center.

As everyone in Vermont already knew would happen, John was tried as a juvenile and adjudicated a "juvenile delinquent". He only spent three years in state custody before being released, just as the law required at the time of his conviction.

Once he was released, he moved to North Dakota, where he spent time in adult prison for possessing stolen property. It was while John was doing his time in prison in North Dakota that he learned of his brother Randy's murder in St. Andrews, Vermont. John would later move to the Gainesville, Florida region of the United States, but he would eventually return to Northern Vermont, and live under an assumed name, where he remains to this day.

In the summer of 1990, around the same time that John had moved to Gainesville, the college town found itself in the grip of terror after five students were murdered in quick succession. The victims had been fatally stabbed, and, in some cases, raped and mutilated, and their bodies posed in sexual positions. One of the victims was even found decapitated.

I remember being contacted by the Florida Serial Murder Task Force that was investigating those serial murders. They had learned that John Pitco was living in their area and were trying to rule him in, or out, as a possible suspect in their serial murder case. They asked dozens of questions about him and the Johnson Street Park attacks. It turned out that John Pitco did not commit the murders they were investigating. They were the work of Danny Rolling, a 30-something-year-old drifter with a long criminal history, who was made infamous when he was dubbed the 'The Gainesville Ripper'.

18

ON JULY 4, 1981, WATERFORD HELD A JOINT INDEPENDENCE DAY celebration and Police Appreciation ceremony at the Johnson Street Park, where this heinous crime had occurred. Aluminum bleachers were brought in and a podium was set up in front of the bleachers. The Park was cordoned off and decked out with American and Vermont state flags. Many of the homemade signs that had been erected around Waterford following the arrest of John Pitco and Tony Hampton had been saved and they were re-erected in the Johnson Street Park as well.

All of the officers, who participated in the May 15th murder investigation, and their families, were personally invited to be special guests, at the Independence Day and Police Appreciation celebration. Governor Snelling, U.S. Senators Robert Stafford and Patrick Leahy were present, as well as Vermont's lone Congressman, James Jeffords. News reports following the event laid claim to the fact that more than thirty-four Vermont State Legislators, the Vermont Commissioner of Public Safety, various Law Enforcement Executives, and too many Mayors, City and Town Managers, Police Chiefs and local politicians to count, attended the event as well.

On the actual day of the event, every police officer who was invited attended, in dress uniform. Those of us who had participated in the investigation were lined up and stood in formation, at parade rest, facing the aluminum bleachers behind the podium. After a host of opening remarks from the officials and dignitaries in attendance, each officer was called to the podium individually, to be presented with a 'Meritorious Service' ribbon, an individual officer plaque, and the applause of the crowd, which was estimated by reporters to number three thousand.

The best thing of all was that Wendy and her family stood beside the podium, and as the Governor read our names and shook our hands individually, Wendy presented each of us with a handshake and a warm thank you.

My family had managed to get seats in the front row of the bleachers, and just when I was presented with my ribbon, Annie stood up and shouted "Way to go, Dad," and Jared stood and called out, "You go, Dad" as both of them waved intensely. I had a lump in my throat so big that I wasn't sure I would ever be able to swallow like a normal person again. They put a smile on my face and made me proud. I stood taller as I walked back to my position in the police formation.

After the Governor had recognized the last officer in our group and the officer had returned to our ranks, the Governor said, "How about a big round of applause to show these officers our gratitude and appreciation for their selfless actions, sacrifices, and dedication to duty." The entire crowd rose to its feet and clapped enthusiastically for nearly ten minutes. This had certainly been one of the most memorable and proudest days of my life.

Many of us would be further recognized, after this was all said and done, by being interviewed on the *20/20 Weekly Broadcast* by Hugh Downs, and would receive honorable mention in a book written, at that time by Peter Meyer, entitled *Death of Innocence,* about this case.

19

Tony Hampton's trial was scheduled to begin on May 6, 1982, in adult court, in Albany, Vermont. I have a clear memory of reviewing the entire case file and reliving the incident yet again, as I prepared for the trial with State's Attorney Jack Banfield.

I was tasked by Banfield with providing the witness list, including addresses and telephone numbers, for each listed witness. All potential witnesses would be considered, and if selected to testify, each would have to be deposed before the trial.

A court-sanctioned deposition is the taking of a witness's sworn testimony. It is used to gather information as part of the discovery process in Vermont, and in limited circumstances, may be used in trial, to impeach the witness's sworn testimony in open court. The witness being deposed is called the 'deponent' and is sworn in before testifying. A stenographer is present at the deposition and records the entire proceeding, along with the witness's testimony. Both the prosecutor and the defendant's attorney are present at the deposition, and may raise objections that are recorded and subsequently decided on, by a judge reviewing the proceeding, and both attorneys may cross-examine the witness, under oath.

With great enthusiasm, I put together the list that the State's Attorney's office had requested because I knew that this meant we were that much closer to convicting and locking up Tony. I was only missing one witness's name and contact information. It seemed that the name of the older, white-haired gentleman whom we had met on the railroad tracks and later in the back of the park when we were searching for and found Stacie's body, didn't appear in any of the police reports. I thought that I had included his name in my report because I specifically recalled writing it in my police notebook. I searched and searched for it in any of the other officer's reports as well as searching my notebook, without any success.

I knew that Officer Jeremy Jones had told me that he had also written down that older gentleman's name and address, when he showed up, walking on the cross-cut path to the crime scene, where we had found Stacie.

I sought Jones out and he reiterated to me that he had written the gentleman's name down. He too thought that he had included it in his police report, but would certainly search his notebook for the name. Jones said he had made a lot of notes since that incident, but that he would take the time to search his notebook and find the man's name for me by tomorrow.

The next day, Jones came to me and said that he was perplexed because he couldn't find that older man's name in his notebook either. We discussed a possible explanation, but could not come up with one. While talking, we both recalled that the older, white-haired man must live in the immediate area of the park because he had gone home and retrieved his yellow rain slicker, before taking his post at the two footpaths in the park, so that he could direct other appropriate responders to the crime scene.

Together we decided that we would go and knock on the doors of the houses in that neighborhood in an attempt to find our mystery man. We drove to the area nearest to the Johnson Street Park, on its eastern border, which was near the area where we had both seen the older man. We had both seen him walk in the direction of these homes when he went to retrieve his rain slicker.

Officer Jones took one side of the street and I took the other. We began knocking on doors, working our way from the homes nearest to the railroad tracks, back towards Johnson and Elm Streets. We agreed to write down the addresses of every house we visited to ensure we had a record of our efforts.

I was optimistic that there was a simple explanation and that one of us would find our older, white-haired witness in short order. Three hours later, we had collectively knocked on the doors of one hundred and seven homes, with absolutely no success.

Several people that Jones or I had spoken to said that they thought that they may have seen someone matching the older, white-haired gentleman's description in the area, back around the time of the Johnson Street attack, but no one knew who he was, or where he might live. Of the people who said that they thought they may have seen him on that day, most of them that we spoke to said that they hadn't seen him back in this area since then.

When we completed our task, I went to Sgt. Green, who was now Lieutenant Green and told him of our plight. He insisted on meeting with Officers Killen, Jones, and me, and we revisited everything that we each recalled about the man respectively. We arrived at no conclusion or plan of action, and after days of back and forth conversations with the Neary County State's Attorney Office about our missing gentleman's name and contact information, there was a consensus that this potential witness had not seen or done anything so unique that the court would insist on his testimony at trial.

To this day, I cannot explain the presence and the subsequent disappearance of the little old, white-haired man. None of us who interacted with him can. I have since heard more than half a dozen people speculate about what they believe about who the man was, and I have several thoughts about him myself. I know he was real, and he was there, just as sure as I was.

Here is the best explanation that I have heard and the explanation I choose to agree with. The older gentleman may have been Stacie Whitcomb's guardian angel. His role may have been to stay with her and guide all of us to her location. We all recalled him as caring and compassionate. His mannerisms and his insistence on helping at the scene made an impression on each one of us that day, and it still does to this day. I can think of no other explanation. I know that we are not all crazy. I have resigned myself to the fact that even if this particular explanation regarding his presence on the railroad tracks and later in the park on May 15, 1981, can be explained in some other way, it doesn't matter to me anymore.

How could anyone explain his name mysteriously disappearing from any police reports and Officer Jones' and my police notebooks? When you couple that with our inability to find him despite our best efforts and our knocking on the doors of one hundred and seven homes, and the fact that some of the people's homes that we knocked on the doors of, said that they recalled seeing him as well on that tragic day, but none had seen him since, no other explanation makes sense.

I say why not. In fact, after years of reflection, I choose to believe that he was an angel of sorts. Even if he was not Stacie's guardian angel, his role and behavior that day was angelic. Thinking that he was there for her makes me feel just a little better about Stacie lying all alone there on the ground on that horrible, rainy day. I don't care what anyone else thinks.

I was anxious about having to testify in Tony's murder trial. This was my first time testifying in a murder trial. Many years later, I would look back and recall testifying in many murder trials, but no trial that was more important or as sensational and closely watched as this one.

On May 6, 1982, I walked into the courthouse in Albany, Vermont, and I took the witness stand. After standing with my right arm raised and swearing to "tell the truth, the whole truth, and nothing but the truth, so help me God", I was invited to sit down. I looked at each one of the ladies and gentlemen sitting on the jury. As I made eye contact with each of them, they smiled reservedly back at me. When I explained what I had done and what I had seen on the day of the Johnson Street Park attack and murder, I directed my attention and comments to the jury.

My testimony lasted for several hours. I described every detail that I could recall—from hearing the call come into the Dispatch Center, to arriving at the scene and my first impression upon seeing "the little girl in the red dress" with her life-threatening injuries. I told the jury about how I was one of three officers who ran along the railroad tracks for three-quarters of a mile before finding the footpath that the train conductor had told us about, where he had seen Wendy stumble from. I also spoke about searching for and finding Stacie under that hideous, filthy mattress.

I could tell that each member of this jury was listening to everything that I said very carefully. By the serious looks on their faces, I got the impression that they understood and believed what I told them.

I got choked up a little when I was asked to describe what I did after we found Stacie and what I had observed. I described kneeling down next to the filthy, bloodstained mattress with the protruding, small feet, and lifting the end of it so that I could check Stacie for a pulse in her carotid artery and when I felt none, I explained how I had gently rolled Stacie up on her side so that I could see Stacie's face, and check further, for any other signs of life. I described Stacie's appearance and injuries in great detail, just as I had been instructed to by State's Attorney Banfield.

I even testified that at the sight of Stacie and her gruesome injuries, I had stood up quickly and walked several yards away from Stacie's body, near a pine tree, hunched forward and had had the dry heaves. I spoke about what the investigation had uncovered and how those "gruesome injuries" were inflicted on Stacie's small body, about my role in the investigation and some of the steps we had taken that ultimately led to identifying John and Tony as the Johnson Street Park attackers. Lastly, I testified about John leading Sgt. Bedard and me to the spot where he and Tony had buried the girls' personal effects and the unaccounted-for murder weapons. I explained to the jury how the spot was excavated and I provided a description of every item we found buried in that hole.

I couldn't help but notice the reactions of some of the jurors, as I testified. The whole time that I was on the witness stand, Tony glared at me from the defendant's table where he sat in his three-piece suit, next to his attorney.

At the conclusion of the trial, Tony was found guilty on all counts. At sentencing, prosecutors asked for a ninety-nine year to a life prison sentence for Tony's role in this horrendous crime. The judge, however, sentenced Tony to forty-five years to life in prison. He also received a fifteen to twenty-five-year, concurrent sentence for aggravated sexual assault.

20

THIS CASE OCCURRED IN THE EARLY AND FORMATIVE YEARS OF MANY of the officers who participated in the investigation careers. Many of those officers would remain in law enforcement until they were eligible for retirement. Some would make personal choices to walk away and do something other than law enforcement for the rest of their lives, some would be promoted and others would move on to something bigger and better.

Police Chief Terrance Whitmore would retire after twenty-nine years of service with the Waterford Police Department, as would Detective Sgt. Bob Green, after having been promoted to Lieutenant and completing twenty-five years of service.

Corporal Fields would be promoted several times during his thirty-two-year career in municipal policing in Neary County, twenty-five years of which would be served on the Waterford Police Department, before accepting a Police Chief's position in another Vermont community, where he would serve honorably for an additional fifteen-years before retiring.

While attending the FBI National Academy in 2002, then Lieutenant Ben Fields, who was the Commander of the Criminal Investigation Division for the Waterford Police Department now, was tasked with reconstructing and presenting a criminal case review and an offender summarization of the 1981 attacks in the Johnson Street Park.

Ironically, the FBI Agent/Instructor who assigned Fields that class assignment had been an FBI Field Agent in Vermont, at the time of the 1981 incident, and he and Fields had worked on the Johnson Street attack investigation together. His name was FBI Agent James Sears, and he had been one of the FBI Agents temporarily assigned to the Waterford Police Department, to assist with the investigation. After Lt. Fields completely reconstructed the case and the offender profiles, he had to present it to the full class for review and consideration. His conclusions and findings would require validation by FBI profilers and FBI Academy Teaching Staff. After careful consideration, it was agreed that Lt. Field's reconstruction and summarization were correct.

John Pitco and Tony Hampton were sociopathic killers. The FBI defines a sociopath as someone who has an antisocial personality disorder (ASPD). Sociopaths can't understand other people's feelings. They often break rules or make impulsive decisions without feeling guilty about the harm they cause. Sociopaths use "mind games" to control friends, family members, co-workers, and even strangers. They may also be perceived as charismatic or charming. While not all psychopaths are serial killers, psychopathy, or at the very least, the possession of psychopathic traits, is a common denominator among serial killers, sex offenders, and most violent criminals.

Before the Johnson Street Park attacks and murder, the FBI had never documented a single incident where two sociopaths participated in the same crime, as co-defendants. A careful review and analysis of this particular case would suggest that this only happened because of the suspects' age and emotional maturity.

Tony Hampton was classified as the dominant, organized sociopath in charge of the plan and the execution of the attack. It was further determined that Tony was a sex offender with a sadomasochistic paraphilic disorder.

Sadomasochists enjoy sexual activity in which they receive or inflict physical or mental suffering on another person. They derive pleasure from inflicting or receiving pain—sadism and masochism combined. Paraphilic disorders are recurrent, intense, sexually arousing fantasies, urges, or behaviors that are distressing or disabling, and that involve inanimate objects, children or non-consenting adults, or suffering or humiliation of oneself or the partner with the potential to cause serious harm.

John Pitco was classified as the less-dominant, disorganized sociopath with sadomasochistic urges, combined with Autism Spectrum Disorder. You will recall that earlier in this book, Autism Spectrum Disorder was described as a condition related to brain development that impacts how a person perceives things and socializes with others, causing difficulties in social interactions and communications.

None of this provides any excuses for either of the suspect's behavior or conduct, but it helps us to understand what Tony and John's roles were, and how they functioned during the attack at the Johnson Street Park on that rainy, day in May 1981.

Sociopaths tend to be very intelligent, but are egotistical loners who are uncompassionate. They lie, break laws, act impulsively, are manipulative, callous, hostile, deceitful, impulsive, lack empathy, and do not feel remorse for their actions. Sociopaths are people with an antisocial personality. Any act of kindness or compassion by a true sociopath is learned and insincere behavior that is practiced to fool or manipulate others.

Some of the most infamous sociopathic killers in history include: **John Wayne Gacy**, who was a friendly man who threw popular block parties, volunteered in local Democratic politics, and often performed as a clown at local children's parties. But Gacy, who had already served a stint in prison for sexually assaulting a teenage boy, was hiding a horrific secret right beneath his neighbors' unseeing eyes. In 1978, police obtained a search warrant for Gacy's house. There they found a 4-foot crawl space beneath the house, which emitted a penetrating odor. They were shocked to find the decomposing bodies of 29 boys and teenagers that Gacy had raped and murdered. Gacy admitted to killing several more men, disposing of their bodies in a nearby lake. His attempts at presenting an insanity defense failed, and he was convicted on 33 counts of murder, and executed by lethal injection in 1994.

Another sociopath, **Jeffrey Dahmer**, committed his first murder in 1978, when he was just 18. He would go on killing until his arrest in 1991, after an African-American man escaped his clutches and hailed down police near Milwaukee, Wisconsin. When the victim led the police back to his captor's apartment, they discovered photographs of dismembered bodies, the severed heads, and genitalia of several other men and a tub full of acid that Dahmer had used to dispose of some of his 17 victims.

Ted Bundy, who was handsome, well-educated, and brimming with charm, Bundy seemed the unlikeliest of serial killers. Which made his decade-long, multi-state killing spree all the more surprising. Following a difficult adolescence, Bundy graduated from the University of Washington—and soon embarked on his murderous spree, killing his first victim in Seattle in 1966. Focusing primarily on attractive college co-eds, Bundy committed a series of murders across the Pacific Northwest. He continued to Utah and Colorado, killing several more women before being arrested. Despite being convicted of kidnapping, he managed to escape police custody not once, but twice, while awaiting trial in Colorado. He moved to Florida, where he killed several members of a sorority and his final victim, a 12-year-old girl who he raped and murdered.

The most infamous of all was **Jack the Ripper**, who was an unidentified serial killer active in the largely impoverished areas in and around the Whitechapel district of London in 1888. According to a study in the *Journal of Forensic Sciences,* the man known as Jack the Ripper was likely Aaron Kominski, who was, a 23-year-old Polish barber who emigrated from Congress Poland to England in the 1880s. He was described as violently antisocial, exhibited destructive tendencies while at an asylum for a short period. On more than one occasion Kominski had to be restrained to his bed.

21

I HAVE OFTEN THOUGHT ABOUT STACIE, HER FAMILY, AND WENDY and her family, but my mind has also forced me to occasionally think about Tony and John.

What would have happened if Tony had escaped detection and apprehension immediately following the Johnson Street Park attack and murder? Would he have committed other similar attacks, rapes, and murders? Would he now be an unidentified serial killer, leaving a trail of murdered victims in his wake? Would he have remained in Vermont, or might he have relocated to other parts of the country where he would start all over again?

Knowing now, what we know about Tony and his personality characteristics, any one of these scenarios, or all of these possibilities might have come to be a reality, were it not for Tony's arrest at the age of sixteen, cutting his potential killing spree to one victim.

What about John? I sometimes wonder if he has committed undetected crimes under his new, assumed name? Is he preying on young, unsuspecting victims? If he has not yet done anything like that, will he, in the future?

Is it possible that many other, innocent lives may have been lost, if Tony Hampton had not been locked up for the past thirty-nine years? Were some other young lives spared by Tony's years of imprisonment? How many other Tony Hamptons and John Pitcos are out there? How many have not even been born yet?

I guess we will never know the answers to these questions with any scientific certainty.

ABOUT THE AUTHOR

THE AUTHOR OF THIS BOOK SPENT FORTY-SIX YEARS WORKING AS a police officer. First in the United States Air Force, and then working in a variety of positions, for several municipal departments in the state of Vermont.

He was honest, dedicated and hardworking. He was described by his peers as one of the "ten percenters" and "over achievers", quickly advancing, being promoted and receiving recognition for meritorious service and outstanding achievements.

During his forty-six-year police career, he spent twenty-four years as a detective, a detective sergeant, a lieutenant, a commander in the criminal investigation division. For the last fifteen-years of his law enforcement career, the author was an accomplished and celebrated Police Chief in Northern Vermont.

The author attended college on nights and weekends during the time that he spent serving as a police officer, obtaining an Associate Degree in Criminal Justice and a Bachelor's Degree in Criminal Justice and General Business Management. The author is also a graduate of the FBI, National Academy, Class of 2002, Section 208.

He is a happily married family man, with four adult children and five grandchildren. He plays the guitar and loves to vacation with his wife in the Caribbean.